Hidden In Plain Sight

The Blackstones

Peter Edward White

Acknowledgements

Beth Perman and Alice Flynn, for being enthusiastic readers and encouraging me to pursue this.

To Madeleine Hutt for her endless patience.

To my best friend Dunk Mclaughlan, for being honest yet constructive.

And to my Wife Jocelyn, for being an amazing sounding board and putting up with me during this obsessional process.

Front cover artwork is by the amazing Christopher Crawford,

www.christophercrawforddesign.com

And images used courtesy of www.unsplash.com

All rights reserved.

Copyright © 2023 by Peter Edward White

All rights reserved.

No portion of this book may be reproduced in any form without written permission from the publisher or author, except as permitted by U.S. copyright law.

Contents

1. Country Roads — 1
2. The Next Day — 6
3. H.I.D.E — 15
4. Dark Places — 23
5. Difficult Questions — 33
6. Secrets and Lies — 38
7. The Study — 44
8. The Wheatsheaf — 54
9. St Bernards and St Bottley's Hospital — 66
10. A Close Shave — 72
11. The Promises we make — 82
12. Read all about it — 87
13. Wrongs for Rights — 90
14. One Giant Leap — 97
15. London Taaaaaan (Town) — 105

16.	Covering Tracks	114
17.	Bonded by Blood	119
18.	Have a Banana	133
19.	Just So...	143
20.	Eyes on the Prize	152
21.	Left for Dead	156
22.	As Above, So Below	165
23.	Clarity	180

1

Country Roads

William woke up as the car buzzed over the rumble strip marking the exit for Amblefield. He knew they were almost there when his phone lost signal, as it always did, and the podcast that he was listening to had cut out.

He had been asleep for at least an hour and in that time the sun was almost put to bed. He had become bored of counting cars among the backdrop of tall trees and listening to his parents bicker about the everyday things they disliked about each other; lack of money, the rent, the car, and of course, William. When William woke they weren't arguing anymore, but weren't speaking either. The open passenger window filled the car with a breeze and added to the tension.

Amblefield was a picture postcard English village. The type you see in the movies where people say things like "Good morning!" and "After you!" while opening doors for each other. It had two pubs, a duck pond, and a village shop that still closed on Sundays, near a very old church that dated back to the twelfth century. They drove through the village, past the shop and up the twisty hill where his granny and grampy lived. As they pulled into the large horseshoe-shaped drive the white timber front of the house revealed itself in the setting sun. The ivy had grown a lot since the last time they visited and glowed almost purple in the red hue.

Grampy must have heard the car coming from a mile off. The exhaust was louder than most and he was already stood waiting on the drive. The catalytic converter had been stolen a few months back by some scumbag while William's dad was in the job centre; *another* failed attempt to get a job. He still didn't have a job so couldn't fix the car and when the eviction notice letter hit the doormat, it was all a bit much really. So, Lindsay Fairchild had decided to do what he'd always done in times of crisis: go home.

"Lindsey, darling!" Granny cried, arms outstretched to William's dad, ignoring everyone else including William.

Grampy put out his hand to shake Williams like an old school master, "You have grown my boy." It's true. He had just turned twenty, a late bloomer, but he had gained a lot of height and width since he last saw him.

"Now, William," he said to him sternly. "Have you been working hard?" William nodded as much as the lie would let him.

"Did you get the birthday card I sent you?" Grampy whispered.

"Yes. Thanks for the cash." William whispered back.

William had been completely preoccupied in the last couple of years with the discovery of parties, that the prospect of having to study anymore was quite unappealing. He was in his last year of university. At a cost of £9000 a year, plus living expenses, he'd be starting his working life at twenty-one with a degree in fine art, no work experience at all, and more than £30'000 in debt. All he had read about is how this country was bouncing from one recession to another, and that graduates are working in supermarkets, as they are the only places still hiring that pay a living wage.

"I'll get the bags then, yeh?" William shouted, as everyone else had already walked up the steps and into the house. His parents were ignoring him, and his dad was enjoying being the centre of attention for a change. He opened the boot of the car and seized the handles of the two rather large suitcases. One was new and black, but the other was an old brown one, covered in coloured stickers from various countries. He tilted it to see more of the labels, but as he did so the handle snapped off in his hand, sending the case into the gravel with a crunch. The case balanced on its edge for a split second before opening like a clam on the driveway, regurgitating its contents all over the place.

"Argh!" he shouted, and looked up at the crimson sky like he was expecting to be struck by lightning. That's when he saw them. A pair of eyes and brown curls of hair. He was being watched by a neighbour in the house opposite. The head disappeared rapidly and the light was turned off moments later. He turned back to the case and all the clothes now spread out on the drive, opened the case and straightened it out to pack things back in. Inside the case on the top lid were some weird symbols and letters hand-painted on with quite some skill and care:

H.I.D.E

He was confused for a second, but could feel the spit of rain starting, so he packed the case and wrestled it up to the house as fast as possible.

2

THE NEXT DAY

"Good morning, William," Granny said curtly, as he walked down the stairs and into the kitchen for breakfast. She was cracking eggs into a bowl, a mere two dozen as usual. William's Granny, for all her faults, loved to feed people, and William loved their house. It had a beautiful entrance hall with a cuckoo clock, light fittings with crystals hanging from them, and an old oil painting of a colonial era military man with one hand stuffed in his waistcoat, looking like he really needs to sneeze. probably from Granny's constant dusting.

The kitchen was huge with a rustic farm table that had seated twenty at a push. A big green and black oven took pride of place in the centre, and it always had something either in it or on it, bubbling away, filling the ground floor with the most appetising smells.

William was the first down, so he had to deal with the stilted conversation with his Granny alone while she made a breakfast big enough to feed most of the village. He placed his book on the table face down.

"So, how is, erm, school?" she asked, frying a half a pig's worth of bacon in the pan.

"I'm twenty, Granny. I'm at uni now," said William, with as much politeness as he could muster.

"Of course you are dear, of course. So, erm, tea?"

"Yes please, Granny." He stared at his phone willing it to suddenly find some signal, but nothing happened. She poured a cup of tea for him into one of her fine bone China cups and set it down on the table in front of him.

"Erm, so…"

Here we go again.

"How long are you staying for this time? Or shall I ask your Mum?"

William's mother was always better at dealing with Granny. The years of wear from her barbed comments had created a thick, impenetrable skin.

"Just a week, I think. Just a week." he said.

William's dad came shimmying down the stairs with an urgency, already with his finger pointing, so he knew that this would not be good.

"Good morning, darling!" Granny beamed cheerfully from across the kitchen, her mood dramatically improved by his mere presence.

He looked at her briefly and said, "Hello, mother," cheerfully and bashfully, before turning his pointing finger to William, the smile falling away like tissue in the rain. The weight of his stare was uncomfortable.

"Why did you leave our new suitcase out in the rain yesterday, hmm? And the other one now has no handle. Gone! Completely!"

"Sorry."

"That doesn't sound like much of a sorry."

William's dad has always been obsessed with apologies, even more than fixing the problem itself, and he will make you repeat the sorry in multiple ways until he believes it. These days William knows the game, so he makes him really work hard for his apologies. There was the time when he was five and happened to be playing with his dad's keys and locked him out of the house, with himself inside. Or the time when William was ten and he removed one of his car wheels as he'd seen how to do it on the telly. He guessed he must have nipped to the kitchen for a snack when they showed the part on how to use the jack.

Oh, and the most recent one; William enrolled his dad into becoming an Avon representative! He'd seen the adverts with the promise of regular money, flexible hours and wonderful in-house discounts. Being a bloke with a name like Lindsey was a blessing in a female dominated industry. You should have seen the look on the Avon area manager's face when William's dad opened the door.

"Lindsey Fairchild?" she'd asked.

"Yes!" he'd said, thinking he'd won the postcode lottery. Her heavily moisturised face sank.

Alas, he didn't take that job either. 'Wasn't the right fit.' He said that a lot and William often thought, *well neither were most of your clothes,* but he still wore *them* until they were threadbare. William can still flick his angry switch from one to a hundred with two simple words: "Avon calling." Today was not a day for the angry switch.

In the light of a brighter day pouring through the kitchen windows, William could now see the damp patches on his dad's shirt, and trousers too. It took all his inner strength to stifle the chuckle that was building inside of him and made its way up and out of him like a tick in the form of a "PAH!" Fortunately, at that exact moment, his grampy was at the foot of the stairs. He walked into the kitchen closely followed by William's mother.

"Good morning, gentleman, sleep well?" said Grampy, as he wandered over to Granny who was standing by the oven, spatula in hand, tending to the black pudding.

"Don't point, Lindsey." He locked eyes with William and winked. He had the most piercing green eyes that didn't look like they belonged to a man of his age. They both nodded and his dad put away his finger at last.

"I'll deal with you later," said William's dad. "And get that crap book off the table."

Grampy kissed granny briefly on the cheek and took his place at the head of the table. "Sorry I was late down, I was on the phone to Cherri, she's been away on business again."

William's aunt Cherri was a bit of a mystery. William had only met her twice, once when he was six and then again when he finished secondary school. He gathered that she was only a few years older than his dad, but a very different character all together. A highflyer you might say. Always jetting off somewhere for a business deal or opportunity. Granny didn't even ask how she was, which he thought was odd; she was obviously too fixated on getting the hash browns to stack.

"So, what's the plan for today then, son?" Grampy asked, looking at Lindsey, just before he bit into his first doorstop piece of toast.

"Carol and I were planning on a walk up to the grove," said Lindsey, as Granny piled his plate. William's Mum sat down with her coffee. "Maybe some lunch by the canal?" she suggested as she stirred, knowing full well that William's dad wouldn't spend a penny on unnecessary things like that.

"Then tonight," said Lindsey, with a pause for maximum effect. "It's Steve and Maxine's party! Steve Macintyre? You must remember Steve, Dad?"

"Oh, yes," Grampy said. "How could I forget the gangly lad with the... you know... issues," gesturing awkwardly to his trousers. Steve had engrained himself into the memory of Grampy forever, by constantly needing a wee.

Years ago, when Steve and Lindsey were younger, Grampy had caught him weeing in the garden all over Granny's rose bush, and once he even saw him wee up the side of the garage behind the car. That was twenty-five years ago, but if the wind is right, Grampy could swear that rose bush *still* smelt of asparagus.

"I remember that time he weed in the vase at that Christmas do. Here's hoping for a drier night tonight," William's mum said, wearily.

Steve and his wife were having a big party tonight. It was their wedding anniversary and they planned to do it in style. They had met fifteen years ago on the hard shoulder of the M1 near Birmingham. Steve had pulled over in a rush to have - you guessed it - his tenth wee in a bush. Just as he was walking back to his car, she rolled up behind his with a flat tyre. He offered to help, and that was that.

That wasn't really that. He couldn't undo the nuts either, but he waited with her for the AA to arrive. What a bloody hero. Fifteen years on, they now lived in one of the new houses on the edge of Amblefield; the ones referred to by the locals as "modern" and "ghastly." Funnily enough, those would have been perfect names for their two children, who were the most entitled and spoiled brats you could ever meet.

William had also been invited to this party, but he really couldn't face it. The idea of having to pretend that everything was ok and being excited about his future to a number of his dad's childhood friends made him feel like a fraud. he decided the best thing to do was stay at home and see if he could spend some time with Grampy.

"Well," said Grampy, "sounds like an action-packed day," as he drummed on the table. "Say hello to piss pot for me, and his devil spawn."

"ANDREW!" Granny shouted. She slowly regained her composure and calmly spoke as she buttered her twentieth bit of toast. "That's no way to speak about Lindsey's friend, even if his children are truly, truly horrible."

After returning from their walk, showering, and faffing about to get ready, William's parents finally left the house at 7pm and started their walk across the village. The red October sky was already fading fast into the hills and the trees swayed casually in the breeze. Inside, Granny was up on her chair again, dusting in the lounge. She honestly seemed to be happiest when she was cleaning, humming to herself some awful old last-night-of-the-proms, old empire tune that was practically unrecognisable.

"Bum de de buuuum..." *Irritating.*

William was a few chapters into his book when she said, "Why don't you put that awful book down and go and see your Grampy in the attic?" as she made a start on the ornaments on the coffee table. She didn't have to ask him twice. The sound of the clocks in the lounge and hall were driving him crazy anyway as they were slightly out of sync with each other, creating a cacophony of rhythms, like a hive of sewing machines.

He climbed the stairs up to the first floor and looked at all the old pictures in frames that lined the landing. Some of his dad on his own in various nauseous poses. Some family ones: a much younger looking Granny cuddling his dad as a boy, looking truly happy, whilst a younger Grampy had his proud arm around his aunt Cherri as a teenager. She had the same emerald, green eyes. There were no young pictures of Cherri though, which he thought was strange. At the end of the landing, he took the second stairway up to the attic room. At the top of the carpeted stairs was the door that was always kept shut:

His Grampy's study.

3

H.I.D.E

William hesitated for a moment then knocked on the door twice. "Come in," he heard his grampy say from a distance. The door creaked a little at the hinges as he did so, and he closed the door behind him. The attic room was rather large with windows fitted into squared-out dormer sections. An old red wine-coloured rug with chewed tassels clung to the middle of the floor with varnished wooden floorboards either side. At the end of the avenue of bookcases was the desk that his grampy was always sat at. He was busy stuffing some papers into a drawer hurriedly before turning on his swivel chair to face him.

"William, my boy, what brings you up here?"

The study always smelled like a mixture of brandy and cigars - two of his grampy's favourite things - so it was no surprise to William when he stood up, cracked open a window, and lit one.

"Cuban," he said. "A gift from George, one of my oldest friends."

"What are you hiding?" asked William, as he looked towards the drawer.

"Oh...your granny's birthday card," he said, as he wafted the dense initial cigar smoke from his face. William knew that was a lie, but he couldn't be bothered to pry any further.

"Don't you have a party to be at?"

William told him that he didn't really fancy going and said that he had a bit of a headache. He could always tell when he was lying, too.

"Would you like a brandy, William?" He used to use the exact same tone when William was seven and hankering after some ice cream.

"Ok then," he said. Last time he had drunk any brandy was in freshers' week. That didn't end well.

"And how about a game of chess?" his grampy said.

"Why not, it's been a while."

He pulled out a small wicker table from beside his desk and opened a cabinet while William found a stool. He pulled a second crystal-cut brandy glass from his cabinet and poured him a rather large one.

"Any ice?" asked William, but his grampy just turned his head sideways as if to pity him and say, *what do you bloody think?*

"No ice... no ice is fine," said William, coyly.

The chessboard was set down and was just how he remembered it; ivory and ebony squares set in an orange, mango wood. Heavy yet intricately carved pieces were lined up on the board. Andrew preferred to play white, which meant he went first. William remembered playing chess at school and thinking it was the best game in the world. A brilliant blend of psychology, strategy and down-right malice that brought out the best and the worst in most people.

William sipped his brandy. The first few sips literally made him shudder like someone had just walked across his grave. As that calmed down, so did he, and he felt the cosy warmth of it settling in. The chess game started quite quickly, as usual, with a few pieces being lost just to tempt the other into making a grave mistake. When the game slowed and there was more at stake, you could feel the tension rise. William tried to distract him.

"That old suitcase I broke used to be yours, didn't it?" William asked.

"Yes," he said, not taking his eye off the board.

"I noticed some letters painted onto the inside of the lid. H.I.D.E. What do they mean?"

He didn't look away from the board but just said, "Some things aren't all that they seem, and some things you should never forget."

Ever cryptic, his grampy. He is full of interesting and twisted phrases that don't really make sense to anyone but him, like, "A bird in the hand is worth two in the bush." Or "A rolling stone gathers no moss." Or a personal favourite, "Necessity is the mother of all invention!" William thinks that he gets the last one; it means that if you really, really need something, you'll find a way to get it.

He was still staring at the board intensely and William was desperate to distract him from his rook. So, he said something he shouldn't have.

"I'm thinking of moving to London after uni."

Grampy's eyes shot up and fixed on his like never before. The green flash was more of a glow this time. "I see... why on earth would you want to do that?" he said carefully.

"Well, some of my friends will be working in London and I'll find it easier to find work if I'm there, I guess."

Truth was, knowing his parents' situation with the house, the eviction letters and lack of money, they wouldn't have space for him soon anyway.

"London is a very dangerous place to be you know," he said. "I could tell you a few stories if it would help change your mind?"

"Feel free to, but I doubt it will put me off," said William.

"I suppose you're old enough now," he shuffled nervously. "I shouldn't really, but..." he stopped himself short, holding his hands up in defeat. "Let's keep this between us, eh?"

William agreed and he poured some more brandy into both glasses.

"You know that I lost my father in the war?"

"Yes, Dad used to tell me. That must have been hard?" said William.

Grampy began, "If I think hard enough, I can still remember being carried down the steps of Bounds Green tube station by my mother. We waited in silence in the lower depths as the bombs could be heard exploding all over London. The walls shook and the noise was deafening, bouncing off the hard tiled surfaces and echoing throughout the tunnels. I'd never been so scared, but we survived. I was eight when the war ended, and with my father no longer with us it was just my mother and I. She had to work to support us, and that meant I had some freedom. Growing up in the rubble of London and having all the bomb sites to explore was a joy to behold. We found so many wonderful things abandoned by people in their houses. Some rooms were completely untouched with laid tables, chequered cloths with crockery and cutlery all set for dinner. Others were not so fortunate, with hardly anything left. Or, in some places, everything would be soaked and peeled around the edges.

The fire engines must have worked all night to put out some of the fires that threatened to engulf the city. One day after school when I was about ten, my friend Ed and I had found a way into a locked bomb site near Mornington Crescent tube. It was an old Georgian house with large, shuttered windows, high ceilings and fancy architectural features. Obviously owned by a rich family. The back of the house must have taken a direct hit as the two rooms on the top floor were missing. Like they had been cut out with a bread knife for all the world to see. Similar to a doll's house.

At the back of the house on the ground floor there was a door that looked like it was just a cupboard. We would have left, but there was a cold draft that was coming from underneath the door. 'Is it a pantry?' Ed asked. The door was stuck fast so we had to find something to jimmy it open with. Ed cut his hand quite badly in the process but wrapped it up in a clean-ish tea towel that we found on the kitchen side. I wish we went home then... I wish that every day."

Back in the study, the wind suddenly picked up and the window was flapping about in the breeze, banging against the dormer's edge. Grampy stood up and closed and latched the window, drawing the curtain too.

"Was getting a bit nippy in here anyway," he said.

William felt cold too, but he wasn't sure if it was the wind or the creepy story.

"Where were we?" asked Grampy.

"The cellar door," said William.

"Oh yes, that's right. We should have gone home."

4

Dark Places

Grampy sat back down in his chair and picked up where he had left off.

"The door to the cellar was now open and hung off one hinge. We found a couple of candles and a box of matches in the kitchen drawer, lit them, and headed down the stairs slowly into the cellar, feeling quite nervous. Once down there, there wasn't much to see to be honest. Some old classical records that were now ruined by damp and a set of old rusty golf clubs. The only other thing was a single shelf on the furthest wall with a black ornament on it. The material was something I'd never seen before, like black glass, and even amongst all the damp and dust, it still sparkled in the candlelight. It was like the dust knew something we didn't.

"The figure was of a man leant against a rock, but he had the legs of a sheep, torso of a man, and a human head with ram horns. His index finger of his left hand pursed against his lips as if to say *'shhhh'* and his right hand stretched out towards us with a little dish, barely big enough to fit a farthing on. I touched the dish to see what it would do, but nothing happened. On the shelf next to it was a miniature fountain pen, which I thought was odd. It was only when I pulled the lid off I realised that it wasn't a pen at all, but a very sharp knife the size of a scalpel. 'What do you think this is?' asked Ed. 'I have no idea.'

"Ed's hand must have been throbbing now from cutting it on the door. 'How's your hand?' I asked, as I pointed towards the blood already seeping through the tea towel. 'It'll be ok. I'll live,' he said.

"I handed him the pen/knife and he went to place it back on the shelf, but as the corner of the blood-soaked tea towel touched the little dish, the eyes of the figurine glowed red. We jumped back. The whole shelf started to vibrate quietly, and the outline of a door started to appear in the stonework around it. We had set something in motion and had no idea what would happen next.

"We moved back towards the stairs of the cellar and watched while the stone door opened inwards quite smoothly, leading to an impossibly dark tunnel. Looking at each other, we couldn't believe what we had just seen.

"We felt the cold air rush into the cellar from the dark tunnel, nearly putting our candles out. I shielded mine so fiercely I almost burnt my hand. Egging each other on, we moved towards the opening, but it was so dark that the light from the candles didn't seem to be able to penetrate the blackness.

"I went first, over the threshold and into the void with my candle held out front like a shield. Ed followed closely behind. So close in fact that I could feel the warmth of his breath on the back of my neck and the smell of smouldering hair as his candle strayed too close to my head. 'Sorry,' he whispered. I was so nervously excited about where we were going that I didn't even care.

"The tunnel was remarkably dry for something so old. I could feel the indentations of the flagstones beneath my feet. The tunnel turned to the right and then carried on for what felt like ages... and that's when we saw it. There was an opening at the end.

"When we reached the end of the tunnel it opened out into a main chamber. The air felt instantly cleaner, and the light from the streets above raised the overall light level. It was coming down from opaque glass blocks set in the pavement that was very high up, with occasional long shadows caused by pedestrians walking above. *They have no idea what's below them*, I thought.

"As we walked into the chamber, we could see that there was a whole network of tunnel openings that all seemed to meet at this very point; at least twenty or so. The largest tunnel was up the far end, and this was lit by torches held near the walls by iron chains. Someone was here.

"Curiosity got the better of us as we crept quietly towards the torches. The flickering light illuminated the carved elements that stood out of the stonework; too many symbols and faces to understand the meaning of it all. Halfway down the torchlit tunnel was a heavily protected wooden door reinforced with metal, but we could hear talking and laughter. The only way we could tell what was on the other side was to look through the keyhole halfway up the door. Ed looked first, for what seemed like forever. I waited for him to say something, but he fell silent, and all the colour seemed to drain from his face.

"He moved over silently like he'd seen a ghost and stared at the wall behind us, blankly. So, I looked through too. Inside the room was a dinner party. The plush red candlelit room looked like it belonged in any five-star hotel, with huge silver framed mirrors on the walls, mink furnishings and a chandelier fit for a king. Bottles of champagne and red wine were dotted around the table with silver service waiters tending to the guests' every need.

"The diners were all in black-tie attire and the women were dressed like film stars. They all seemed to be wearing an item of silver jewellery with a single black stone. Some had rings, and others bracelets or necklaces. All with the same type of black stone.

"I was still confused by Ed's reaction until I saw a middle-aged blonde woman opposite who asked the man next to her to pass a bowl. As he did so, I saw the bowl was full of fingers. Little fingers with knuckles and nails. Bloodied at the ends. These were *not* ordinary people. I didn't know it at the time, but these people were the worst type of people you could hope not to meet. These people were ritualistic Satanists. Blackstones. And on the menu today were what looked to be body parts... body parts of babies.

"They all seemed so calm and happy, like it was a celebration of some sort. 'Leg anyone?' said a young man sat in the middle. 'Oh yes, me please,' said a young girl sat opposite him.

"The clink of glasses and laughter was at odds with what I could see. The man directly in front of me laughed as he pretended to try and steal food off another diner's plate, blood dripping down from his chin. As his gaze moved across the room his eyes suddenly fixed upon mine at the keyhole. It felt like an electric shock. It was like he could see into my soul.

"I lurched back from the door and inhaled deeply with panic. I felt sick. Ed still stared at the wall blankly. We both sat there in silence. We needed to get out of there, so I pulled a shell-shocked Ed up onto his feet and headed back towards the main chamber.

"We moved through the chamber as quickly as possible, looking for the tunnel we came in from. They all looked the same! Why didn't we mark it? *So,* so, stupid. I trusted my gut and chose one.

"With our candles held tightly, we walked once more into the pitch-black tunnel and headed back towards the house, but it felt like this tunnel twisted in a different way. At the end of it there was a similar arrangement, though. It was just a simple shelf, with a knife this time, and a small black glass dish. I did the honours while Ed held our candles so I could see. I made a small cut on my little finger and squeezed it to let a drop of blood drip onto the dish. The door began to shake.

"As we waited for the door to open, the air moved, and our candles blew out. Those few seconds in the pitch black felt like an eternity. The door opened inwards and into a clean cellar that didn't smell the same as the first one in Mornington Crescent. Ed handed me my candle and I relit it quickly and stepped into the new cellar. I turned around to look at Ed still standing in the doorway.

"I tossed him the box of matches and remember seeing him trying to strike a match as a large, cloaked arm appeared out of the blackness and contorted around his neck. I looked on in terror as he gurgled once and vanished into the black, while the door rumbled shut behind him. I was now truly alone and petrified. I had to get out. Now.

"There were two flights of stairs out of the cellar. I got halfway up when I heard the stone door open up again, and a deep voice said, 'Get him.' I ran to the top of the stairs and opened the door out onto the street. It shut quietly behind me and when I turned around it didn't look like a door at all. No handle, just the side of a concrete railway bridge opposite the little park at Harrington Square. How on earth did I get here?

"I ran for as long as I could before my chest burned and my legs hurt. Doubling back a few times just in case I was being followed. By the time I ran out of steam I was in Somers Town, walking up towards Camden Road, holding the side where a stitch had developed a few streets back.

"My mum worked at the bakery near the tube and would be finishing her shift soon. I waited for her at the bench out front as I sometimes did, and we walked home together. 'You're quiet today, good day at school?' she had said. 'Ok,' I had replied. 'Just ok?' she enquired. 'Yeh.'

"That was my first introduction into the darker forces of the world," Grampy said. He rested both of his hands on Williams, reassuringly.

"What?!" he said. "Really? Are you having me on, Grampy? You must be."

He couldn't believe what he had just heard. He'd read all sorts of ghost stories and strange tales on the internet, but this... this was in a league of its own. His grampy waited for him to settle a bit before letting his hands go.

"What happened... what happened to Ed?" William asked eagerly.

"No one really knows but I never saw him again. The police came asking questions in the neighbourhood, but I noticed something that made the hairs on my arms stand up. Both of the policemen had small silver signet rings on their little fingers with a single black stone. Exactly the same kind that I saw in that room. So, I lied. I said that Ed and I were supposed to meet up after school at a bombsite in Kentish Town, but he never showed.

"His mother put up posters for months. Every time I saw the picture of his face it made me feel sick. That last look on his face before he gurgled and rolled into the black void has stayed with me forever."

"What happened to her, his mum?" William asked.

Grampy's tone saddened, "Later that year there was a gas leak in her house; No survivors." He picked up the brandy glass and with one meaningful gulp, drank what was left. He upturned the glass like a town fair magician and gestured with his free hand, as if to say, *vanished*.

Sounding vengeful now, he said, "Who do you *really* think runs the world, William?"

5

Difficult Questions

"Governments, I think..." said William, hopefully.

His grampy made the noise from the Family Fortunes TV show when a family member guessed a wrong answer: a grinding two-tone buzz.

"The politicians? The media? The corporations?" said grampy, sarcastically, that grinding two-tone buzz again.

"All puppets. There are darker forces than you would believe at play here, and in most cities, but acutely in London. And how do they control the masses? P.R.S," he said.

"The music royalty people are Satanists??" William asked.

"No, no, you silly boy. Listen to what I tell you. My god you really are your father's son sometimes. There are secret societies all over the world, William, but all the ones that you can read about freely online or in most books are red herrings. Decoys, if you will. The real ones have members from all walks of life - from the politician to the butcher, from a banker to the police, fire service and even scribes. The common red thread that binds them is the need to bring about change the only way they've ever known: dark magic.

"This involves rituals and sacrifices to appease their spiritual rulers; keepers of their souls, which they sold willingly long ago for a promise of a more fruitful life. Blinded by their faith and by greed. Many people in power are blackmailed into joining the cults and bent to their will, usually attacking their weak spots with drugs or sexual temptations. Once they have evidence, they will exploit it to control even the most determined or stubborn of mind. Then, once the right people are in place, P... R... S. **Problem. Reaction. Solution.**

"**The PROBLEM** is the thing they can create through various means, whether it be a mass shooting or serial killer, an outbreak of disease or terrorist attack. They have mind control techniques they have perfected over the last century and unlimited resources. The mainstream media is always at hand for full coverage.

"The REACTION is the perceived outcry of the public, often overstated massively by the mainstream media, for something that must be done to stop the same thing happening again.

"The SOLUTION is *the outcome* they wanted all along, whether it be tighter restrictions, a lowering of regulations, acquisition of natural resources, or even a war. Very profitable, war, especially if you finance both sides. War is often used to mask the true intention, but they make money out of it anyway.

"This is how it works." he said,

For an older man, he was quite the performer.

"You want something another country has, but your hands are tied legally from just taking it. So, you create a situation where terrible atrocities occur in your country, including the loss of innocent lives and blame it on *that* country where the thing you want is. The media does its job and spreads the message far and wide. People are outraged. They want justice. So, you declare a war on that country, having to borrow millions or billions to spend on arms. Head over there for some retribution with the full backing of your nation and any other allies, just to take what you really wanted from the country in the first place. Simple.

"The things to remember and to look for, my boy, are *the accounts*. *Always* follow the money. Who does a government borrow money from? When they say a nation is in debt, to whom do *we* owe? Tick.

Who owns or has shares in the arms companies that supply the war machines and accessories? Tick.

Who stands to benefit from the acquisition of natural resources or assets from the invaded nation? Tick.

"Connect the dots and you will usually find they are all the same people. Names concealed deeply within guilds, foundations, trusts and giant corporate enterprises, of course." he took a very dramatic seated bow.

"Woah... woah," William said. "What does this have to do with London, Grampy?"

"Everything, my dear boy, everything. It's where it all began. Are you sure you still want to go?" His green eyes were watery but sincere. It was the look on his face as he said it that repeated in William's mind.

They had finished their game of chess and even though William had won, he still felt like he'd lost. He wasn't sure if it was the brandy or unhinged conversation, but he felt quite tired, so he decided to head to bed. He said goodnight to his grampy and headed back down to his room.

He couldn't sleep. His head was spinning with all those stories. He thought of grampy's friend Ed, being swallowed by the dark, and his ten year-old grampy, a kid with bright green eyes running for his life.

Who really runs the world? He thought.

Pictures and TV clips of politicians played on a loop inside his mind, while a two-tone grinding sound dominated his imagination. He was so relieved when his mind gave up the fight and let him slip away to sleep.

6

SECRETS AND LIES

William woke up with the sound of someone retching in the bathroom next door to his bedroom. It was his dad, Lindsey. In between the horrendous noise was Granny trying to comfort him.

"Better out than in darling."

—- curdling splashy noises —

"Well done dear."

—- deep, curdling ploppy noises —

"That was a good one, so proud of you!"

William had heard enough. He skipped past the bathroom, down the stairs and into the kitchen where his mother was brewing a pot of tea, looking a little worse for wear but partially smiling at least.

"Morning, Mum, good night, was it?"

"Depends on your definition of good, I suppose," she said dryly. "Your father decided to join Steve and Maxine's magical whiskey tour..." she feigned amazement. "Which basically consisted of them standing around the drinks cabinet all night, drinking far too much whiskey and talking about how cool they used to be, which I assure you, they *never* were.

Piss-pot Steve had passed out by 11pm and had wet himself, and Maxine the energiser bunny kept going until her batteries fell out at 12; after your delightfully drunk father puked up the handful of chipolata 'canapés', right into her cleavage. 'These are brand new!' she screamed, as she stomped off upstairs not to be seen again that night. Meanwhile, I got lumbered with ensuring the survival of their awful, self-righteous offspring all evening. Bloody brats."

William loved his mother when she was hungover. She lost her filter and just said things straight. As the morning dragged on, the filter was being rebuilt bit by bit, but was toppled occasionally by his granny. Granny had put

Lindsey to bed again after his vom-athon and checked in on him every five minutes. She was also troubled that William's mother couldn't seem to care less about her precious little boy, but was quite enjoying being needed by him for a change.

A pathetic noise could be heard from the direction of his bedroom, "Water... agh... please."

"Mummy's coming, Lindsey."

Pathetic.

It was Sunday, so Grampy had already drunk his coffee and left the house at 8am to play golf. He did this every week as part of his routine, so he certainly wasn't going to miss it just because his idiot son and family decided to descend upon them. He knew It was only a matter of time before Lindsey cornered him to have a 'chat' about borrowing some money, again. Grampy could feel it in his bones, so he decided to let off some steam before the thought of his irresponsible son ruined his swing.

Considering it was October it was actually a nice day. The sun was bright and clear in the sky, and their well-kept garden looked happy. The red Acer tree stood proudly halfway down the garden and its leaves looked vibrant in the sun. William's mum, Carol, decided the best course of action was to take her tea, book, and headache tablets, outside for some fresh air. William, on the other hand, had other ideas. He had his breakfast and headed back upstairs to shower and get changed. Luckily his room had its own en-suite, as he could hear the vomiting start up again while he showered.

"Well done, darling!" said Granny.

Once changed, he headed upstairs to the attic room but the door to Grampy's study was quite clearly locked from the outside by a combination padlock with four numbers. "Bugger," he said, under his breath. He went back to his room to lay on the bed to think. "Necessity is the mother of all invention," said William, in his best Grampy tone. Pointing his finger he said, "Some things are not what they seem, and some things must not be forgotten." He chuckled to himself, but then it hit him:

H.I.D.E

Some things are not what they seem, and some things must not be forgotten.

"What if these for letters stood for something? Could it be...?"

William counted out the first nine letters of the alphabet and wrote them down:

A B C D E F G H I

He then added numbers underneath:

A B C D E F G H I

1 2 3 4 5 6 7 8 9

It couldn't be that simple, surely...

H = 8

I = 9

D = 4

E = 5

8,9,4,5...

He felt a tingle in his stomach; he had to try.

His dad was now asleep and snoring in his bed. It was 11am, and according to his mother, Grampy wouldn't be back until at least 2pm. He headed up to the attic room once more and to his surprise, his granny was coming out of the study with empty cups, brandy glasses and a few plates.

"Hello, William, just taking the opportunity to, erm, clean, while your grampy is out at golf,"

she said.

The four numbers in a line on the open padlock that hung off the clasp were very clear to see. 8945. William was right! A small smile gathered on one side of his mouth. Not that it mattered now.

"8945?" He asked.

"Yes, dear. He uses that same combination for *everything*... memory isn't what it used to be these days."

I beg to differ, Granny, he thought. *There are things I bet he'd give anything to forget.*

William lied and said he had left his phone charger in the study last night and needed to grab it.

"Be a dear and lock the padlock when you leave, and don't linger. You know how funny he gets about people being in his study." She hurried off down the stairs, arms full, to carry on with her chores.

Bingo. William was in.

7

THE STUDY

William stepped into the study like he was walking on ice. He wasn't quite sure why, but it felt so wrong to be in there without Grampy present. He was even more aware of the noises the floorboards made as he walked down the room. They creaked slightly in places as if to send a message to anyone downstairs that he was up here, looking into things he shouldn't.

He headed straight for the desk and opened the main centre drawer that he saw Grampy stuff some papers into. On top of a pile of newspaper cuttings and old crosswords was a birthday card in a bright pink envelope, stamped and addressed, but it was to Cherri Fairchild, not Granny, somewhere in London. Luckily, the glue on the envelope had not stuck very well, so William opened it without causing any damage. The card had a drawing of twelve red roses on the front, some glitter, and a huge italic scrawl that simply said *Happy Birthday*.

How original, he thought. Just then, a Grampy-ism popped into his head. 'Sarcasm is the lowest form of wit, dear boy.'

"Sorry, Grampy," he muttered to himself. He almost had second thoughts and put it back, but curiosity got the better of him. He began opening the card just to see if he'd written anything inside. Two newspaper clippings slipped down onto the desk.

To my dearest Cherri,

It's still not safe for you here. Lindsey is here to ask for more money again. I wish he had even half of your tenacity.

Reading in between the lines, London is crawling with activity.

I'm trying my best to cover your tracks.

I have the book you needed. It's deposited here:

SDB 104

Cuthberts Bank.

392 The Strand

London

Something to reflect upon: face + hide

A.

X

That's a strange sign off, thought William, as he set it down on the desk to take a picture of it. Why not, 'Dad'? Or 'Your father?

One of the newspaper clippings that had slipped from the card was face up on the desk:

American Tourist missing in London: Wife pleads for any information.

It had a picture of a slightly plump man in his late fifties, dressed in beige cords with a white short-sleeved shirt and bum-bag. In the wife's statement to the police, she said, "He had gone looking for what he considered to be a local landmark he'd seen a few days previously. A large black house near Upper Thames Street. Blackest thing he ever saw... kept repeating it over and over." By that evening, he still hadn't come back and no one has seen him since. She reported his disappearance the following morning after a sleepless night.

The other newspaper clipping was face down on the desk and had *P.R.S* written in black biro, with the *P* circled in red. *Problem*, William thought. He flipped it over and the headline stated:

NHS: At breaking point

There is a public health emergency arising in London, as the average waiting time for a doctor's appointment is extended to three weeks in some boroughs.

An anonymous GP told us, "We have a record number of immigrants presenting themselves for medical treatment at this time, and we are struggling to cope."

It went on to talk about the delay in routine operations. What did all this mean? What on earth was his aunt Cherri really doing in London that required such secrecy?

William took pictures with his phone of all the bits he had found to study later and carefully placed the card with the clippings back into the drawer exactly the way he found it. He decided the best thing to clear his head would be a walk down to the canal. He left the study and closed the padlock as requested, rolling the numbers to a random combination. Down the stairs, he then grabbed his coat and was out of the door at last, the autumnal air filling his lungs. He hiccupped once and recognised the taste of brandy in the back of his throat.

That was a weird night. The look on Grampy's face still lingered in his mind, as well as the sound of his voice. "Are you sure you still want to go?"

He walked down the hill towards the village shop while a girl was walking up. From a distance she looked rather quirky, wearing denim dungarees, a pair of green wellies and a multi-coloured tie-dyed hemp thing.

As they got close enough, he saw she was around his age. She had beautifully smooth dark skin, curly brown hair and lovely eyes that twinkled in the sun. She was quite attractive but obviously a bit shy, as she couldn't even look him in the eye when he said, "Good afternoon."

She didn't even slow, just said, "Hello." with a polite but tight smile and carried on up the hill to the house opposite his grandparents'.

Hang on a minute, William thought, *She must have been the one spying on me on the night we arrived!*

HIDDEN IN PLAIN SIGHT

He carried on down the hill to the shop, even though it was shut, just to look in the window at the local ads. Bit of a tradition for him, as they always made him chuckle - a far cry from the type of ads they had back at home.

Lost: *Sheep*

Quite large, black mark on right hind leg.

Smells a bit like damp and cat wee.

Last seen near Porters Bridge.

Please call: *The Wheat Sheaf Arms and ask for Sean.*

Classic! William took a picture of that one.

Job vacancy:

Oddbods Dairy Farm.

General farm hand.

Duties includes the early shift, preparing the cows for milking and clearing down the gulley's behind.

Only the strong willed and hardy need apply.

A sense of smell or humour will not be necessary.

Ask Jim the milkman for an application form.

Brilliant. Can you imagine doing that? *'Click'* went his phone.

Apprentice opportunity:

Bonnson and Jehovah: Horologists

Makers of fine clockwork mechanisms and stunning timepieces.

Apprentice required to learn all aspects of the Horology trade.

A keen eye is essential, and some experience using hand tools would be a distinct advantage.

Salary: negotiable.

TIME WASTERS NEED NOT APPLY

Enquiries on Monday only

William walked towards the duck pond when a duck hopped out of the water, waddling right in front of him, and started pooing all along the water's edge. It went on for ages and he couldn't work out why. He was opposite the pub just as he jumped back in the water to join his quacking friends. The local pub had lots of locals sitting outside in the autumn sun, sipping beer and ordering food. The smell of the beer made William feel a bit queasy as he passed, so he stepped up the pace and headed down the lane.

So many beautiful buildings were in Amblefield. It's listed in the Doomsday Book for one reason or another. Local folklore states that King Henry I was passing through the village on his way to London and decided to relieve himself in a bush. The house that bush now partially obscures has a blue plaque nailed to it to state the fact. The owner, a rather chubby man called Ralph, had it commissioned himself, but no one, especially visiting folk, needed to know that. In a world full of uncertainty, on a nice day like today, there's something you could bet your hat on - he'll be outside his house, on a wooden step ladder, polishing that bloody plaque.

Maybe Steve piss-pot Macintyre is of royal stock after all, William thought. *I wonder how perky he is today after last night's party.*

William passed an old, thatched cottage that stood proudly on the corner of the lane, and noticed the little straw animals woven into the ridge. Each thatcher has their own signature mark, so they could tell who thatched that building last.

When he finally made it down to the canal, everything, including his thoughts, slowed down.

He walked in silence, listening to the birds arguing in the trees and fish splashing in the canal. Peace at last. There was his favourite spot further up by the lock that had a bench overlooking the drop. He sat down, took out his phone, and looked to see if by a miracle they'd erected a cell phone mast overnight, only to be disappointed again. He looked through his pictures instead.

A few snaps of his hungover mum "waving" at him in the garden. Not using all her fingers either. *Well, that's just rude.*

The pictures of the shop window ads made him laugh again, always did. The thatched animals, the canal, the card, then the newspaper clippings. He read the American tourist one again.

Black house... Upper Thames St.

It didn't really register the first time in the study, but now it caught his interest.

So, did the American guy find this house? And is that where he went?

William didn't know, but knew a way to try and find out. He needed to access the internet somehow. So, he decided to do what the locals did: go to the pub.

8

THE WHEATSHEAF

The pub was busy outside. Some barmaids were collecting glasses, while others were handing out pints of ale from little round trays. "Thanks love, but you spilled a bit," one man said, who seemed to be covered head to toe in what can only be described as bird poo.

"Don't get shitty with her," his mate said.

"Bit late for that! Look at the state of me!"

"I told you not to sleep by that pond." The whole table erupted with laughter, with ale being spilled everywhere and crisp packets falling to the floor, only to be set upon by Stan, the pub's resident Jack Russell, who was really enjoying his afternoon and all the crisps that fell to the floor.

William managed to get past the squad without drawing any attention to himself and slipped inside the pub where the contrast was like night versus day. Quiet and peaceful. Yes, you could still hear the general commotion outside, and the occasional eruption of spilled drinks, but much better.

There were only two people in there, not including the staff. One older gentleman of a similar age to William's grampy was sat at a table on his own; flat cap and cane next to him, a half-drunk pint of ale sat precariously close to the table's edge, and he was reading the Sunday Times. The other man was sitting on a tall stool at the bar. He was in his early thirties, a bit tubby but dressed smartly. He obviously had a thing for one of the barmaids, as every time they left the bar he was checking his hair in the reflection of his phone, propped up against one of the beer pumps. William walked up to the bar and waited for the barmaid to return from a drinks delivery. She walked in through the door and just let out an audible sigh, composed herself, adjusted her top, and walked back behind the bar.

"What can I get you," she said, with the exact same smile all barmaids have, which implied, *I might be single, I might not be. Buy a few more drinks and you might find out... you might not.*

"Erm, pint of, erm..." *God, I sound like Granny.* "Bitter, please."

The barmaid paused. "Masons?" she asked.

"Er... ok."

"Coming right up."

It all happened so fast.

She grabbed a pint glass and used the middle beer pump. Only trouble was, the smartly dressed guy's phone was propped up against that one... not anymore. As she pulled the pump towards her the phone seemed to defy gravity and slid up the pump handle, and as she forcefully pushed the pump handle forward to go for another pull it launched the phone into the air, spinning almost as if in slow motion, across the bar and straight down into the elderly gentleman's pint glass with a *kerplunk*.

The chap at the bar spun on his stool to face William, arms outstretched in anger, "What did you choose Masons for?! Nobody with half a brain drinks that shite."

Well, it's probably because I have more than half a brain, William thought.

At that moment, his phone started to ring in the pint glass. It sounded like the music they used to play at Butlins when you were under the water trying out your new goggles. The angry man wandered over to the old man's table and apologised extensively for getting his phone in his pint. William could see him recounting how it happened with massive arm movements. Then he was pointing towards William and shouting "Masons? Masons..." to which the old man just said, "This is Masons. I quite like it. Good day," and returned to reading his paper.

"Hello," the angry man said whilst answering his soggy phone, bitter dripping down in lines on his face towards his chin. "No, I'm not under water. I'm not. It's not gone well. No, I'm not down a well! I said it hasn't GONE well. Hello... hello?" He walked outside and William felt some relief. He heard the same word *Masons* and the outside table erupted again. This time two or three glasses smashed, and the laughter carried on for ages.

"Thanks for that," the barmaid said, "I've been trying to get rid of him for ages. Every Sunday he comes in and just stares."

"I think he must like you."

"Wow... you think?" she said sarcastically, "You're not from around here, are you? Where did you come from?"

"I live in Perinsgrove, just outside of Barchester. It's a bit different than here. Bit rougher."

"Bigger," she said, starry eyed.

"Crowded," said William, trying to be realistic.

"Exciting," she said, looking out into the distance hopefully. William gathered that she'd outgrown this village and needed to get out.

"Grass is always greener I guess," he said awkwardly. "Erm, do you have WIFI here?"

"Yes, we do. It's snail pace but it's better than nothing. Code is on the board," she pointed towards a blackboard above the bar whilst grabbing her little tray, adjusting her smile and walking back out to the front line.

Finally, he thought. William sat at the back of the pub in a darker spot to keep out of sight from anyone who may enter the bar, found the network and entered the password.

'Password1234.' *Really? Come on.*

It worked and he was soon receiving about thirty Whatsapp messages all at once, which seemed to turn his phone into an alarm clock. *Ding, ding, ding, ding.* He scrambled for the temporary silence button, hit it, and sighed. Bloody thing. The phone wouldn't let him search until all the notifications had come through. Anti-social media, more like.

Once it had finished and calmed down, he went on to the map application and typed in *Upper Thames St, London.* The map opened and zoomed into the part of London where Upper Thames Street is. It was in the City, not just London; the square mile. That took him back. William was thirteen and in the garden with his grampy when he first learnt about the City of London.

"London *is* the city, I hear you cry!" He was like a Shakespearean actor. "Ah ha. I know something you may not know. The City of London is a city, within a city. You see?"

"No, not really," thirteen-year-old William had said.

"The City of London, otherwise known as 'the Square Mile', is the original Roman settlement of 47 AD that they called 'Londinium.' They built a wall around it over the next couple of hundred years. By 410 AD the Romans had

had enough and decided to go home. The empire was in decline, the weather turning bad, and the city was now mostly deserted.

"In 886 AD the Anglo-Saxons re-occupied the walled city and began to breathe some life into the cold stone fort it had become. Alfred the Great made sure that Lundenburgh, as *he* named it, thrived. With a lot of manpower, he set about making the city a place of wonder and laid down a new city street plan. He managed to repel the Viking raids that had become a regular occurrence, and stood strong against any enemy that dared to walk up to the walls.

The Vikings learnt not to bother, the Picts learnt too. People learnt and as a society, evolved. So did the city. London, as we know it today, grew around the walled city and spread far and wide. As the years passed by, the strength of the City of London endured.

The walls have come down bit by bit, and sometimes the only giveaway that you have crossed the border, can be a small coat of arms with a red cross on the street signs, but it's a different place altogether. The size of the population that actually lives there is less than 10,000, but Monday to Friday a staggering 500,000 people are employed there!

The boundaries are marked by stone or metal dragons holding a medieval style shield, which looks like a St George's cross. If you look closely enough, you'll see a sword in the top left-hand corner. This supposedly depicts the sword that beheaded Saint Paul, whom the massive cathedral was built to honour.

It has its own laws, own police force, fire department and hospital. It has its own Lord Mayor who rides in a beautiful, gilded carriage and wears ceremonial clothing, while the Mayor of London just wears a suit like any other businessman.

They have a representative that sits in the Houses of Parliament while in session, that doesn't conform to either wing, called the Remembrancer. He is *not* an elected MP. He is there to ensure any decisions that are made do not adversely affect the City of London's interests. It also happens to be one of the most influential financial capitals in the world. Even the Monarch has to ask permission to enter, but I'm not sure how true that bit still is.

"There are two other places in the Western world that hold a similar position and privilege. Do you know where they are William?" he asked.

"No, I don't," William had said bashfully.

He stretched three of his large fingers out and pulled them down with the other hand for dramatic effect.

"Number one - The City of London." He pulled one finger down.

"Number two - Vatican City in Rome, home of the Sistine Chapel, painstakingly painted by Michelangelo, and many other exquisite pieces of art. It is also the smallest sovereign state in the world, protected by the Swiss guard. Its vaults are said to contain more lost knowledge than anywhere else on earth." He pulled another finger down.

"Number Three - Washington DC in America. *D.C* stands for the *District of Columbia*." He pulled the last finger into his fist.

Columbia is derived from Christopher Columbus who is credited for the discovery of the new world. He didn't actually land anywhere near North America and initially thought he had landed in India, hence why they called the indigenous population at the time *Indians*. Americans know full well how to make something wrong seem right just by being loud and repetitive. Washington is named after one of the founding fathers of the USA and, after its revolution and subsequent independence from the British, its first president, George Washington. The USA has fifty states; Washington D.C isn't part of any of them and stands proudly as their capital.

"Think of all three as a triangle," Grampy said.

"A triangle... like a pyramid?" asked William.

"Exactly. You have...

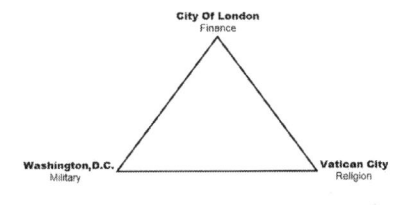

Triangle of Power States

The City of London – Finance.

The Vatican City – Religion

Washington DC – Military

Some people think that they are all secretly controlled by just one group of people," Grampy said.

"Really? Why would they want all of that?" William had said, naively.

"Why, indeed," said Grampy.

Why would anyone want all that power?

Just then William's phone rang. It snapped him out of his daydream memory and scared the crap out of him. It was his mum. "Bill, where are you?"

Uh oh... he knew something was up. They only ever called him Bill when trying to keep him calm.

"I'm at the Wheat Sheaf, using the WiFi, what's up?"

"It's Grampy, he's been hit by a stray golf ball. We're driving to the hospital. Pick you up on the way, in a minute."

Oh my god... poor Grampy.

He downed his bitter but left a few sips, placed the almost empty pint glass back on the empty bar and ran outside past the rabble who gave out a "Whaaay! Where's the fire? Ha ha!" More beer and crisps flying everywhere.

William could hear his dad's car coming before he could see it. The throaty noise got louder as the little car careered down the hill towards the pub. As it came closer, he could see a very worried Granny sat in the front passenger seat with her hands on the dashboard and eyes shut tight as he screeched to a stop outside the pub.

"Get in!" Lindsey shouted out the window. He looked less green than the last time William saw him, albeit a bit sweaty. William climbed in the back of the car with his mum, and they wheel-spun up the road, leaving a large black cloud outside of the pub and smashing a few empty glasses in their wake.

"Whaaaay!"

He really hoped his grampy was ok.

9

ST BERNARDS AND ST BOTTLEY'S HOSPITAL

Lindsey's driving could only be described as 'erratic'. Granny had to sit in the front as she suffered from terrible car sickness. This journey was no exception, and her face was the same shade of green as the downstairs loo, which clashed with the pink overcoat she was wearing so badly, that even Andy Warhol would have blushed.

They were about ten minutes into the journey when William overheard his Granny say, "Slow down Lindsey darling... Mummy feels... *Barrff!*"

Ever tried attaching a hose to a tap that was already on full bore? That was Granny's white leather gloved hand as she tried to stem the flow. The dash of the car was being sprayed in regular pulsing intervals with this morning's full English. It was all in the air vents, dripping down into the door pockets, the radio, CD slot, and even all over the gear stick.

William and his Mum wound down their windows as fast as they could in the back before the smell of the mushrooms reached them. Lindsey slowed down to a steady 75mph, face completely void of any emotion and just said, "Well done, Mum. Well done."

The rest of the journey was in complete silence with all four windows down to their stops. They pulled into the hospital car park around 3pm and followed the blue signs for short stay parking. Lindsey parked incredibly badly, as usual, taking up almost three spaces, and Granny got out of the car. To William's surprise, she didn't have a single mark on her from the carnage twenty minutes ago. Now they were stationary the state of the car was really on show.

"Burn it, just burn it," uttered William to his mum as they got out of the car. She smirked, but did not respond, as Lindsey was already looking at the board for parking regulations. He was spinning around like a confused compass with his hand over his brow, almost like a Pirate of Penzance.

"Meter? Has anyone seen a meter? No meter?"

"It's done by a parking app, Dad." William shouted across to him. "I can download it now if you like?" William looked at the board for the details: *Extortiopark app - The expensive way to park in a rush.* He was just about to start the download when his dad said, "It's ringing, it's ringing. I would prefer to speak to an actual person, William," as he held his index finger aloft. He began walking around in a three metre circle like someone who really needed the toilet.

William's mum just rolled her eyes before starting to walk up the hill towards the A&E, and William joined her. Granny too, but you could sense her resistance to leave without 'her Lindsey.'

"Bye bye, darling, Mummy loves you." she mouthed, as she walked backwards up the slope, the invisible apron strings pulling tightly, no doubt.

As they reached the summit, William could still see his dad doing his strange toilet walk down at the bottom, but decided to concentrate on what was important: Grampy.

The automatic doors to the A&E opened with a metal screech and they walked through into the reception area. It was quite a large room with a V shape of desks in the middle that resembled the bridge of a star ship, only this was made of Formica and scuffed, dusty Perspex.

Sunday was a quieter day for the hospital, as most of the chairs that surrounded the 'enterprise' were empty. A few chairs were taken by a high-viz-ed workman with his arm in a sling, two teenage girls giggling whilst taking selfies, and a young lad who had appeared to have superglued his hand to the bald spot on his dad's head. He did not look impressed and was ignoring his son's repeated requests for a hot chocolate from the overpriced vending machine.

"Name and issue," said the large woman, robotically from behind the grotty Perspex at reception.

Granny leant in towards the Perspex delicately and began to say something when the large lady boomed,

"Get back behind the yellow line!"

The force of her voice alone was enough for all of them to take two steps back.

"Name and issu" came the monotone robot voice again, thankfully slightly quieter.

"Andrew Fairchild. Golfing, erm, accident," announced Granny.

"Bottley Ward. Report to nurse Alice. Go." Her attention had now immediately shifted to the people coming through the doors in full medieval re-enactment wear.

William and his family walked up the hall following the signs for the Bottley Ward and into the elevator that happened to be open and waiting.

"Get back behind the yellow line!" could be heard emanating from the reception area just as the elevator door closed tightly in front of them, muffling the clangs of metal as all the men dressed in armour jumped back.

The elevator must have been called by someone on the floor above, as it slowed as quickly as it got started, opening to reveal a young male doctor fixated on his clipboard. He looked up and William's mum, Carol, let out a small squeak. Granny tutted at Carol in her usual way. Carol always had a thing for doctors. William remembered getting home from school and having to watch hours and hours of Grey's Anatomy. After a few weeks he could recite every episode of seasons four to ten, line for line.

The elevator slowed to a stop, the doors opened, and they all stepped out on the fourth-floor lobby and followed the signs for the Bottley Ward off to the right. As they reached the ward, everything was quieter and warmer.

They were met by a nurse at the desk who had a strong Yorkshire accent and light blue, twinkly eyes. Granny moved towards her reluctantly, waiting to be shouted at again. She relaxed a bit when she realised another bomb wasn't about to go off and asked for nurse Alice.

"That's me!" said the lovely nurse. They were all relieved.

"Andrew Fairchild, please," Granny said, with a little more noticeable emotion as her voice quivered. She had had a traumatic day after all.

"Are you relations?" she asked, kindly.

"Wife and family," Granny proclaimed proudly.

"Certainly, follow me."

10

A Close Shave

The nurse led them down through the quiet and calm ward. Some of the cubicles had their curtains open and you could see various people sitting in bed, some with family around asking questions, another man with a heavily bandaged hand reading a book, holding it up with his good one.

They got to a cubicle with all the curtains drawn around it.

This must be Grampy's, William thought, *He hates hospitals, always has.*

The kind nurse opened the curtain just enough to slip through and talk to her patient.

"You have visitors, Mr Fairchild."

"Call me Andrew, please, I insist." Grampy said, in his wonderfully calm tone.

The nurse opened the front curtain in one swoop and there he was; Sat up in bed, mug of tea in hand and a whopping great bandage on the right side of his head, with a little blood weeping through.

"Oh, Andrew." Granny said, as she hurried to his bedside, trying to work out how to give him a kiss without hurting him anymore.

"Hello my love." he said, descending softly. Carol and William stood at the foot of the bed in silence for a while, while they had their moment.

After a minute, Grampy looked up and said, "So how did you get here so fast?"

Granny answered, "Lindsey brought us, dear, in the noisy little car. The journey was a bit... bumpy."

"Lumpy, more like." said William, under his breath. His mum smacked him on the thigh.

"So, where is he, then?" Grampy asked.

"He's still trying to pay for parking, I think." said Carol.

"I had better call him and tell him what ward you are in." She stepped out of the cubicle and walked towards the lobby, so she could make a phone call without disturbing the other patients. Grampy set his empty mug down on his bedside table.

"What happened, then?" asked William, worriedly, pointing to his head.

"Well, Gerald and I had just had an awful tenth hole. Disastrous, you might say. I lost two balls and bent my wedge trying to get out of a sand bunker. Gerald poked himself in the eye whilst trying to eye up his putt, then tripped over his bag, causing him to badly twist his ankle.

I decided the best course of action would be to head back to the clubhouse, borrow a buggy, then to go back and collect Gerald. It was quite far from the clubhouse, being the tenth hole, so I decided to take a few shortcuts through the wooded areas to speed things up. It was going well, and I was making good progress until I emerged from some trees, onto a fairway and then BANG. Next thing I know, I woke up here."

"Oh," William remarked, in sympathy.

"Oh, actually...is Gerald OK?" Grampy asked.

Meanwhile, sitting on a log at the tenth hole, Gerald was wasting his time and his phone battery to listen to the talking clock. "The time sponsored by Accurist on the strike of 3 will be 3:47... *Beep Beep BEEP.***"**

"Oh yeh, he's absolutely fine." said William, while Grampy looked around for the water jug.

Granny turned to William and mouthed the words, "I'll call Sally at the club now."

Grampy had found the water jug, but it was almost empty, so Granny seized her chance to make that phone call before Gerald tried hopping.

"I'll go and get this filled up for you, dear." said Granny, with a smile.

"Thank you, my love." said Grampy, as she disappeared off up the ward to find a sink.

The moment she was out of earshot he beckoned William closer and got him to sit down at the chair next to the good side of his head.

"I must ask a favour of you, William, one of the utmost importance. I need you to go to my study, the padlock code is "89…"

"45," William finished.

"How did you know?" he asked, looking at William with surprise. "Actually, never mind, we don't have much time. In the central drawer of my desk is a birthday card."

"Yes, you said before. Granny's," William said, - knowing full well it was actually for his aunt Cherri.

"Well, I may have a small confession to make." he mumbled, "the card is for your aunt Cherri. It's signed, sealed and ready to be posted, and I was going to do it today, but then this happened," he points to his head. "It's imperative that it finds its way to the post box ready for collection first thing tomorrow."

He placed his hand on William's shoulder and leant even closer. "Can I rely on you?"

"Yes, of course, Grampy. I'll post it as soon as we get back later."

"There's a good lad." His eyes hadn't lost their twinkle even though it was obvious he was slightly sedated.

In the meantime, Carol had seen Granny wandering off with the water jug and decided to make sure she didn't get into any trouble. She followed her down a long corridor with doors either side. She watched as Granny turned the corner heading towards the utility area. Just then, a double automatic door opened on the left and a massive laundry trolley was pushed out by an orderly. They immediately turned left and headed in the same direction she was walking. But as they did so, a white doctor's coat fell from the trolley onto the floor at her feet.

She picked it up with two fingers to inspect it just in case it had blood or something worse down a sleeve, but it must have just come out of the laundry as it was clean and dry. She looked around for somewhere to leave it. Just as she neared the end of the corridor, next to the door marked "Female Changing 401 F60", was a full-length mirror.

"Really Carol? Are you really going to do this," she said to herself. *"Yes, Carol, yes you are!"*

With that, she swung the coat around her shoulders like a cape, pulled her arms inside and out through the sleeves, with jazz hands outstretched. She spent the next few minutes pretending to walk past the mirror, stopping to talk to herself. "Oh, Dr Carol, thank you so much for saving my life the other day!" "All in a day's work little lady," in the best John Wayne impression she could manage. She took out her phone and pretended to have a call. "Yes, Grey, it's Dr Carol. 30ml of adrenaline and get them into an OR stat," she spoke out loud.

Just to her left, she heard someone say, "Dr Carol, is it?" She froze with fear but tried not to let it register. She turned on her heels to face the nurse. She was in her fifties with her hair tied back, cold brown eyes and an upside-down watch on her left breast. Blood was running down from her hands and dripping off her elbows onto the mottled green floor.

"I have a patient in the Bottley Ward that really needs some help. Please come quickly."

"Ok," Carol said. "Show me the way."

What have you done, Carol? You stupid cow!

While Carol was otherwise occupied, Granny had found a little kitchen in the utility area. She washed out the jug and began filling it with fresh water. As it neared the top, she pushed the lever to close the tap, but it sheared off. Water was now coming out of the top of the tap in an arc and already creating a puddle on the floor by the dishwasher. "Erm, erm, erm..." she said, while picking up the jug and walking back towards the Bottley Ward in a hurry, splashing water onto the floor from the jug she was carrying.

She made it back to the lobby just as Lindsey, her son, was stepping out of the elevator. "Hello, darling, manage to pay the parking thingy, did you?"

"Well, sort of," Lindsey said. "The man on the phone wanted to know what number space I was in, which was tricky as I was in three! Took me half an hour just to straighten the car up. *Very* tight spaces here."

Granny didn't really understand a word and just said, "That's good dear, well done." before splashing some more water from Grampy's jug on the floor between them.

"How's Dad?" he asked.

"Oh he's fine, Lindsey. He's this way."

As they walked into the Bottley Ward, there was a cubical immediately on the left that had its curtains drawn. He could have sworn he heard Carol, his wife, say, "Oh that looks painful," but dismissed it when he caught sight of his dad at the far end.

"Lindsey, my boy, you made it," Grampy teased.

"So did you, just about, by the looks of it," he retorted.

As Grampy started to retell the story to all those who missed the previous performance, Carol had managed to sneak out of the first cubicle. She slipped the robe off quickly and popped it into the laundry basket by the nurses' station to re-join her family just as Grampy said, "Bang… next thing I know, I woke up here." Everyone ooohed, mmmmed and ahhhhed, so Carol joined in.

After a while Grampy seemed a bit tired so they said their goodbyes in turn, and all walked down to the lobby to wait for the elevator. As they passed the nurses' station, the angry nurse was on the phone. "Yes, can you ask Dr Carol to report back to the Bottley Ward immediately. What do you mean, *'who'*?"

Carol was the first in the elevator, funnily enough, and let out a sigh as the doors closed. On the ground floor they stepped out into the reception. It looked like the green room of a Lord of the Rings film set. Knights in full armour trying to sit in the funny little chairs, while one of them had a single arrow, sticking out his arm at 90 degrees. To top it all off, there was now a leak raining down from the ceiling tiles above straight onto the head of the angry robotic receptionist, who had to resort to using a ring binding folder as a makeshift umbrella hat.

"Get back behind the yellow line!"

11

THE PROMISES WE MAKE

Back in Amblefield, they pulled into the drive once more at about 6pm. It had been a much calmer drive back, and nobody really spoke at all. The smell from the incident earlier was still present and the car was a mess, but even that didn't really matter in the grand scheme of things. Grampy was safe. That alone was enough for them.

They got out of the car and walked back into the house. Granny got started on the dinner. William's mum and dad went to use the showers and William decided to fulfil the promise he had made to Grampy. He ran up both flights to the study, unlocked the door and walked over to the desk to open the drawer.

Cherri Fairchild

Apartment 4

Chiltern Mansions

106 Old Montague St

Whitechapel

London

E1 5NU

William lifted his t-shirt and wedged the card in the top of his jeans before covering it again, and headed down the stairs into the entrance hall to grab his coat. He remembered that there was a post box next to the shop at the bottom of the hill, so he left the house and headed off down the hill in that direction, removing the uncomfortable card from his jeans as he walked, kneading out some of the creases his belt had made, but had failed to notice the single thread of black cotton now snagged on the corner of the envelope. As he got closer to the shop, he could see people leaving the pub from the other side of the duck pond. *Must be tea-time,* he thought, as he reached the post box.

'NEXT COLLECTION: 0500' was written on the little silver tag.

Perfect, he thought, while pushing the envelope through the slot. Just then, the girl William had seen earlier with the weird clothes said, "Hello again," shyly, as she walked past.

"Oh... hi," he said, rushing to keep up. She was heading back up the hill towards her house, opposite his grandparents', so he decided to walk with her.

"I'm William, what's your name?"

"Jess," she said. "How long are you here for this time?"

Was she one of Granny's spies? he thought but dismissed it.

"Oh, just a week. Heading back to uni the following week, you see." It must have been something in his voice that gave something away.

"Not what you thought it would be, then?" she asked.

The hill started to steepen, making it harder to speak. "Erm... well it is, but I've had enough of studying now. I feel ready for the real world," he said, with a little too much enthusiasm.

"Grass is always greener I guess," she said, with a cute smile. "It rarely is though, is it? Rarely is."

"So, what do you do, Jess?"

"I work at Oddbods Dairy," she said plainly.

If William had taken a swig of a drink, he would have spat it out.

"What, with the sucky things?" He became quite animated, like Grampy would, pretending to stick imaginary suckers on even more imaginary cow teats. "Oh, and the poo! How *is* your sense of smell?" he said, holding his nose.

She laughed, and looked even more attractive as she did so. "You are funny," she said, as she chuckled.

"No, no, I just take care of the admin for them. Mr Oddbod isn't so great with the paperwork, so I get left alone to deal with it."

"That's good, then." he said, feeling slightly out of breath as they reached the top of the hill by their respective houses.

"Right then, William, see you around maybe?" she asked, as she walked up her driveway.

"Yeh, maybe." said William, trying not to sound too keen. *Wow,* he thought, *she is lovely.*

He headed back up to the house just in time for dinner. Granny had already prepared a Sunday roast before she left to head to the hospital. Even though some of the Yorkshires were past their best, the rest was to die for.

That night in bed, he thought of Jess and her smile. He couldn't tell if it was the roast dinner or the thought of her that made his chest feel warm and fuzzy. After that, all he could think about was Grampy. The stories he had told him, the big bandage on his head, and the promise he had made to him. *At least I managed that one,* he thought, and drifted off to sleep as the wind made the trees play shadow puppets with the moonlight.

Back at the post box, a single black cotton thread had snagged on a paint chip near the slot and the letter was now suspended eight inches down inside the post box, spinning like a weathervane in a tornado as the wind blew past the slot. It hadn't reached the bag at all.

12

READ ALL ABOUT IT

The village shop had opened at 6am as usual. Margaret the shop owner was very punctual. You know, a stickler. There was a sign in the shop above the cigarette cabinet that read:

To be 10 minutes early is to be on time.

To be on time is to be 10 minutes late.

To be late is completely unacceptable.

Do your duty, do it well.

Newspapers were all bagged up, ready for the children to deliver on their paper rounds. Floors swept, windows cleaned, and even the cans on the shelves had their labels front and centre. She had arrived at the shopfront at 5.15am that Monday morning in the glow of the yellow streetlamp above her shop. She didn't know why, but she knew something was off.

Felt it in her bones, you might say. The postman had been and gone as usual, she knew that, as he always left a little bit of a mess as he dragged the mail sack out of the old post box. *I'll deal with that,* she thought. But there was something else.

The post box was covered in a light layer of dust, so she instinctively took an old handkerchief out of her pocket and started to clean the dust away, but as she reached the slot, she saw at the corner there was a single black cotton thread caught on a paint chip with its end floating in the air, wistfully.

She looked round to see if there was anyone else around, but as usual, the village still slept.

She gently pulled on the black thread and felt whatever was attached, rise towards the slot, and as it was almost at the top, she reached in with her free hand to retrieve the object. It was a birthday card in a pink envelope.

"Fairchild," she said with recognition after reading the front. "He can't even post a letter properly." she said in disgust.

Being of a slightly vindictive nature, instead of just posting it again she took the letter into the shop, placing it behind the till in full view. She had been on her own for over ten years now since her last husband walked out on her. Since then, she decided that she would be better off alone. In a world out of control, at least the shop would stand to bring some order to all this chaos.

As it was Monday, she knew that Andrew Fairchild would be in at some point later and that she could tease a reaction out of him with it then. She smiled, although not too much. It was far too early for that.

13

WRONGS FOR RIGHTS

William woke up at 9am to a busy Monday morning in the village.

There were tractors charging up and down the hill towing all sorts of different farming machinery. Courier vans and deliveries of all sorts happening around the village. Such a difference from the sleepy Sunday they had just had.

Back at the house, everyone had finished their breakfast and was sorting things out for the day ahead. William planned to stay behind and read while they all went to the hospital to collect Grampy.

Granny was so pleased that he was allowed to come home.

They set off from the house at 11am, and William sat in the garden at the side of the house that overlooked the drive.

HIDDEN IN PLAIN SIGHT

He waved from behind his book as they drove off. That part of the garden also provided a good viewpoint for Jess's house opposite. Not like that mattered or anything.

Just then, as if by magic, she walked out of her front door and waved at him as she walked down her driveway towards the road.

"Why aren't you at work?" he shouted cheekily. "Those invoices won't write themselves!"

"Why are you reading that crap?" she said. "Anyway, I don't work on Mondays. Going to the shop, need anything?"

"Hold on. I'll come too!" he said, leaving his book behind on his chair.

They walked down the hill towards the shop, chatting along the way about various things: his plan to move to London after uni, her plan to maybe start her own business importing festival wear from Nepal. It was nice to see the shop open for a change, and he could really use a cold drink. He liked tea, but not in the quantity his granny liked to make it. He opened the shop door and held it open for Jess, saying "After you." practising his country manors.

"Well, thank you," she said, as she walked past him and into the shop.

"No, no, you really are welcome." he teased, and stuck his tongue out. She giggled.

Just making her laugh made William feel like he'd achieved something for a change, and that everything was going to be alright after all. He went over to the drinks fridge and pulled out a freezing cold bottle of lemonade. "Two for £2, want one?" he asked.

"Ok, thanks." she said, picking up some crisps.

He picked up a second bottle and headed over to the counter to pay.

"Will that be all?" Margaret the shopkeeper asked, as she beeped the bottles with the scanner. "Just a bag please." he said.

"Not a problem." She ducked down briefly behind the counter to get one, and as she did so William saw the pink envelope with Grampy's writing on it, propped up against the shelf.

Oh my god, that's Aunt Cherri's birthday card!

Margaret was back up with the bag, obscuring his view of the card. Before he knew it he had paid, his drinks were in the bag, and she was now serving Jess.

He stood near the door with his head and heart racing.

How did the card get there? Did it fall out? Did someone try to steal it?

He had to do something. He needed a plan.

He and Jess walked out of the shop, and she knew something was up. William explained what had happened about the card not getting posted. She just said, "Just explain and say that you are his grandson? She'll probably give it to you."

"I can't take the chance of her not believing me. She doesn't know me from Adam."

William knew he had to find a way to get it back without her knowing.

"I've got an idea," said Jess. "She sometimes shuts the shop briefly when she gets a delivery. If I go around the back and ring the bell, she will lock the door, turn the sign and be gone for a minute or two."

"But that means I'll need to be in the shop before she locks it?" said William, as he questioned her plan.

"That's right, you will." said Jess, looking determined.

There were already four or five people in the shop at this time. William walked back in just as a man walked out and headed straight over to the magazine rack towards the back of the shop. He had to find somewhere to hide before Jess rang the backdoor bell. Anywhere. There was a thin but tall cupboard by the pet food, so he tip-toed over, keeping his head down, opened the cupboard and slipped inside sideways. William had to straddle a bucket and felt far too close to all the cleaning products on the small shelf in front of him.

"Riiiiiiiiiiing!"

Just in time.

"Everybody out... everyone out," Margaret screamed. "Must be Anderson's," she said to herself. She looked around but couldn't see anyone left in the shop.

"Riiiiiiiiiiiing!" Jess had rung the bell again.

"Coming," she said, whilst forcing the last customer out, shutting the door and sliding a large bolt lock shut. She turned the sign to closed and walking briskly towards the backdoor.

William opened the cupboard slowly, stepped out as quickly and quietly as he could, snuck over to the counter and grabbed the birthday card, noticing the bolt lock on the shop door.

"Bloody knock down gingers," said Margaret from the corridor at the back of the shop.

I'm running out of time, he thought with a panic. He got himself back into the tall thin cupboard just as Margaret returned to the main shop area and placed the poor card back in his belt under his shirt again.

"Well, I'll be bringing this up at the village committee meeting on Thursday. Heads will roll, you can count on that," said Margret, pointing towards the back door. William was starting to see why his grampy hated her.

She opened the shop up again and William heard quite a few people with loud voices walk in. After a minute he opened the door and stepped out of the cupboard slowly, but in his peripheral vision he saw someone looking at him. It was one of the customers, a middle-aged man reading a copy of '*What Parsnip*', so he improvised. He picked up a cloth and cleaned a few shelves with it and carried it towards the back of the shop. The customer lost interest. He made it down the corridor to the back door and left the shop with just a click of the latch.

Phew!

Jess was hiding behind a bush and jumped out when William was near enough for her to see it was him.

"Did you get it?" she asked.

"Yes. Touch and go for a minute."

"Nice cloth. So, what now? Will you post the card again or what?" she asked.

"I can't. It has to get there today." he explained, throwing the stolen cleaning cloth into a bin.

"No point in getting a courier now. It's too late and it'd be really expensive anyway. You might as well bloody take it there yourself," she said jokingly.

That's when it dawned on him.

He was going to London.

14

ONE GIANT LEAP

▽

Jess had very kindly offered to take him to the station six miles away. He had run up to the house to grab some things and left a note on the kitchen table:

Gone out for the day, Back later.

William

x

As he left the house, Jess was already moving down her drive in a really old yellow VW Beetle with one hubcap missing and rust all around the edges of the bonnet lid.

"Nice car." William said, as he hopped in.

"It's a rust bucket but it drives well, and it's saving your bacon." she said defensively.

"Yeh, it is... is it yours?" he asked, trying to be heard over the sound of the engine as they were going up a hill.

"No, it's my mum's. My dad bought it for her on their first wedding anniversary. She had a health scare last year and now walks everywhere!"

"And she lets you borrow it?" he asked, as they levelled off.

"Well, not quite, but this is an emergency. And besides, I couldn't take the chance of her saying no," she said with a wink.

My God she's gorgeous, he thought.

"What about your dad, where's he?" William asked.

"Oh... he died.... a couple of years ago now." she said quietly.

"Oh no, that's awful," he said, just like everyone probably said, when they didn't know what else to say.

William thought to himself in the awkward silence. When anybody dies it's always sad for someone, right? And it seems like when quite an old person dies, people don't feel the sting as much. They say things like, "How old were they? Oh 86... good innings, then." Or "Oh bless, well we all have to die of something, right? What a life they must have had, eh!"

The truth is, when a girl loses her dad at eighteen, and he wasn't even fifty, there aren't snappy phrases for that kind of loss. There are no words at all, really. Every time her mum gets a bad cold she wonders, *Is this it? Is it happening again?* And with every achievement, every defeat, birthday, engagement, Christmas and wedding, there would be a little part of her mind that her dad still occupied that wouldn't let herself enjoy the moment, fearing the sting of his absence. That is what true loss can do.

Jess was a bit quiet for the rest of the journey, and William gathered why. They pulled into the station at around 1pm and she dropped him off quite close to the ticket machine.

"Thank you, you are a star." said William, the silent pregnant pause was quite uncomfortable, but she looked at him.

"Are you ok?" he asked softly.

She didn't say a word, just leant across towards him.

Woah, woah, this is it - we are going to kiss - she smells lovely.

Only her head went past his, and her hand reached out and opened the passenger door by the latch, pushing the door open a bit.

"There's a bit of a knack to it," she said, killing the mood.

"See you later - stay safe. Here's my number just in case you need picking up." She held out a business card. He read the card as she drove away, grinding gears back towards Amblefield:

Jessica Loudwater

Office Administrator

Oddbods Dairy Farm

07-

Just then he heard the horn of a train starting to pull around the bend and slow down into the station. It was his. *Agh.*

He fought with the touch screen terminal a bit before finding the button that said 'Euston, day return.' He tapped his card, collected his ticket, and ran towards the platform. William jiggled down the stairs, ran up the platform towards the train and jumped on the first carriage he reached just as the doors beeped and closed.

Made it, phew.

There weren't many people on the carriage and most people were either reading or listening to something on their headphones. Nobody ever talks on British trains. He always found that strange.

As the train pulled out of Amblefield, he wondered if he was making the right decision. *How crucial is this card?* He took out his phone charger cable from his coat and made good use of the USB outlet near his seat. They even had WIFI. Much nicer than the trains he used back home. He then decided to do some research.

He took his aunt's address from the card and typed it into his map app. It zoomed into a street in Whitechapel, and he saw the closest tube station was Aldgate East. Next search was how to get there from Euston. He saw a map of the London Underground and had a complete meltdown.

"My god, how do people use this spaghetti? I can't even see Euston, let alone Aldgate East!"

A guy in his forties sat opposite him must have felt sorry for him, as he put his book down to say,

"Don't worry mate, you get used to it. Saaaafbaaaand on Northern line, via Bank, change at Moorgate,

Hammersmith and City line, two stops east," he said, in a thick London accent. It was only then that William saw the little pin on his blazer, which was the London Underground logo. The man sitting to his left had one too, only much to William's horror, it had a small black stone set into the base of it.

"Thank you very much." he said, trying not to give his nerves away. "I'll write that down now," he added, as he got a small pad and pen out of his jacket. As he did so his wallet slipped onto the floor face up. His ID was on show. The man with the black stone leant forward and picked his wallet up for him and said, "Fairchild... William Fairchild. Well, that's good to know."

Was Grampy's story true? Was there really a network of these nasty people in London that did horrible things? He looked just like a normal guy reading a book. Grampy's words swam in his head:

"From the politician to the butcher, from a banker to the police, fire service and even scribe."

Maybe he had it all wrong, and the little black stone meant something else, like a manager or something, but something told him in his gut to run. He thanked them. He unplugged his phone, stood up and walked towards the front of the train pretending to look for the toilet. Once he had moved up a few carriages he found an empty table and sat down, facing the direction he had come from, just in case he was followed. He watched and waited a while. Once he felt safer, he decided to carry on searching online.

He looked into safety deposit boxes at Cuthbert's bank specifically. It took a while, but finally he found a forum where a guy was complaining that the access code was only five digits and didn't feel it was secure enough.

Hang on, he thought, *five? I thought it was four.* He looked at his photos of the card again and saw this, something to reflect upon: face + hide

He had completely missed it last time. It was a calculation. William was quite bad at maths, but even he knew that.

So, H.I.D.E was 8945

He drew out the first nine letters of the alphabet again.

F = 6

A = 1

C = 3

E = 5

Face + Hide was 6135 + 8945.

He needed his calculator for this one. He typed the calculation in and got 15080.

5 digits, that's interesting. Shame I'll never get to see if I was right this time.

Just then an announcement came over the speakers:

The next station will be London Euston, where this train terminates.

That was fast.

He was almost there.

15

LONDON TAAAAAN (TOWN)

▼

The train started to slow down as it entered the covered area of the station. It was almost 3pm, but the sun didn't seem to shine as bright in the city and brief showers of rain were quite common at any time of year. The yellow light that lit the covered area gave everything a different hue, making the reds appear brown and the blues greener.

"So, this is London." William said. Not that anybody listened.

Nobody listening would be the recurring theme for the next hour at least. The train came to a gentle, shimmying stop and most of the passengers were waiting by the doors, willing them to open, like greyhounds in a starting box. The person nearest the door is silently entrusted with the responsibility of hitting the open button as soon as it becomes illuminated. Any longer than 0.001 seconds reaction time would be deemed a failure in their eyes and would invoke a wave of tuts amongst the pack. The door bleeped, opened and they were off.

300+ people stepped out of the train carriages and onto the platform all at the same time, like a river had just burst its banks and was heading towards the dam at the bottom. The staff were quite used to this carnage as it happened all the time. William was swept up to the automated barriers in the deluge and saw people tapping their phones and cards on the yellow disks to open them, squeezing through the gates, which immediately slammed behind them, aggressively.

William wondered if wars were like this. Were there people like him, who didn't really want to run at the opposing army forces, but didn't really have a choice? Luckily, he already had his ticket in his hand as he would never have been able to get it out of his pocket in this vice grip of people. Before he knew it, he was at the front. He put the ticket in the slot of the barrier and it appeared again at the top, but the gate didn't open. He felt a surge of pressure rise and fall behind him.

"Upside down," said the man next to him, who was being swallowed by a huge man's armpit.

The wave of tuts dissipating through the crowd to the back was quite unsettling. William tried again with the ticket the other way up. The gate opened quickly, and he was ejected through by the sheer pressure of people behind him, whilst the gate shut on a poor lady. The machine was beeping manically. Another wave of tuts fluttered.

He was free. Now he had a choice. Take the ramp up to the station? Or down an adjacent ramp to the underground? After the ordeal he just experienced, William decided that he needed some air.

He took the ramp up towards the main Euston terminal, and at the top of the ramp, it opened into a huge space with a couple of hundred people facing him in a line, not looking forward towards the platforms, but up.

As he walked further in, he saw multiple screens suspended from big metal brackets showing the arrival and departures of trains. Every now and then there would be fifty people suddenly scrambling towards the platforms, some dragging little cases and shouting the platform number - desperate for a seat, he guessed - only to be replaced by a trickle of another fifty or so that had walked through the doors that led outside.

He headed against the tide and towards the exit, side-stepping people whose whole attention was already stolen by the giant screens, while a busker in a mismatched suit played a heavily worn alto sax along to 'Ghost Town' by The Specials.

Heading outside, the air was chilly and wasn't helped by the cloud cover that seemed to drape over London like a blanket. He sat down on a bench outside, took out his drink bottle and breathed. London, from what he'd seen so far, was too fast, like a hamster on speed, clinging on for dear life to its running wheel. Everyone in a hurry! So consumed by being first that they missed out on the calmness of sometimes allowing yourself to be last.

"Excuse me, Sir." said a man in an oversized coat. "I need help. I've lost my wallet and I need some money to get home. Is there any chance you can spare some change, please?"

Judging by the state of his trainers and dirt on his face, he hadn't been home in a long time.

"Sure." said William, taken aback. He reached into his pocket for some change and producing a £2 coin.

"Thank you very much, Sir." he said. "Have a great day." he added, just like it was an everyday transaction. William half expected the man to ask him if he wanted a bag for his sense of self-satisfaction.

As the man walked away, he wondered how many others like him were in London.

"Oldest profession in the world, begging." he remembered Grampy saying once.

William checked his phone for the time and decided to message Jess, just to thank her again for the lift and say that he'd made it to London. As he did so, he could hear the beggar start his speech to another couple as they walked into the station. They didn't stop and walked straight past him without a look. "Have a great day." he said after them, with a twist of sarcasm and a pinch of salt.

"Some people."

William got up from the bench and prepared himself for another charge, this time it was towards the London Underground transport system, more affectionately known as the Tube.

Nerdy Fact:

The Tube is a network of tunnels and overground sections that run on 250 miles of track, twisting across greater London, serving 270 stations, and with around five million passengers every day. When it opened in January 1863 it was a world first. It was far smaller then but has since grown into a goliath. Pulmonary arteries that feed the thumping heart of the metropolis known as Greater London.

• • • ● • ● • • •

William followed the signs for the Tube and found himself very quickly being ushered onto an escalator going down. Everybody that wasn't walking down was standing on the right, so he did the same. As if the escalator wasn't moving fast enough already, people were still running down the filleted steps on the left while the Tube trains could be heard screeching and hissing in the tunnels nearby.

William remembered what the man on the train had told him, so he followed the signs to the 'saaafff baaand', or southbound, northern line, via Bank. William's ticket wasn't valid anymore as he had only bought a return ticket to Euston, so he was now relying on his bankcard to tap with. His overdraft was already getting a pasting this month, and this wouldn't help.

The platforms were smaller and not as busy, which was a good thing. He even saw a few rats scurrying around, looking for food on the tracks. A distant noise and rush of air was being squeezed out of the Tube on the left and all of a sudden, the Tube train appeared like red toothpaste all along the track, screeching to a stop at the end.

All the curved doors opened with a 'bing-bong' automatically, and people got off and on, as the Tanoy spouted inaudible announcements from battered speakers. William stayed standing by the doors. He only had four stops to Moorgate. Didn't seem worth the hassle of trying to sit down.

"Mind the doors, please, mind the doors." said the train driver over the internal distorted mic.

The tube doors shut, and they moved off with a jerk almost instantly. He didn't have time to hold on to anything, so he ended up flying sideways into the back of another man.

"Oi, watch it!" said the man, angrily.

If looks could kill, thought William. He was quite a tall man in a long black raincoat. So tall, in fact, he clung onto the rail hanging from the roof with ease. The black stone in his signet ring glistened in the pale fluorescent light of the tube carriage.

Oh no, not another one.

"So sorry." said William, and he turned to face the window so he couldn't see the look of the man's disgust anymore. William held on tightly while the carriage swayed through the bends, trying to stay planted on his feet. The Tube moved so fast it was scary. William felt uneasy, like the whole carriage was watching him as he stared out of the window. As they moved through the dark tunnel, he focused on the long runs of cable and equipment all strapped to the wall.

How many of these people were Satanists? One was too many, as far as he was concerned.

William had to be smart about this and not give the game away. Time to get off.

The next station is... Moorgate.

Please be sure to take all your belongings with you as you depart.

16

COVERING TRACKS

William was the first to leave the tube as it opened.

He had already spotted the yellow exit sign, so knew where he had to go.

He sprinted through the tiled corridors and made it to the escalator, flat out. Running up the escalator, he was aware of his hypocrisy, as he'd previously mocked how much of a rush everyone was in. At the top he could smell the fresher air coming from the exits. He tapped out at the barrier and made his way outside onto Moorgate. It was starting to rain.

William saw there was a taxi rank outside, so he decided to get one. A black cab pulled up and a lady was getting out. "Thank you," she said, as she closed the door.

William walked up and the driver said, "Where are you going mate?" through a gap in the window.

"Just a sec," he said, checking the address on the card. "Chiltern Mansions, 106 Old Montague Street, White Chapel, please."

"No probs, not too far. Hop in." he said.

William had never actually been in a black cab before. Surprisingly spacious, and a Perspex screen between the driver and the back cabin. The driver pulled away and the engine hummed. They turned back on themselves and nipped down the little streets behind the station. The turning circle of the cab was amazing, and he really enjoyed the ride. A large counter with a '£' sign and red characters totted up quite quickly as they travelled.

"Busy day so far?" William asked, as the cab went over some bumps. They had reached the end of the street and it was at £4.20 already. "Ouch." he said, as they went over another bump.

"You are my last job, mate. Been out since 6am and I've had enough now to be honest.

First time in London?" the cabby asked, looking at him from the rear-view mirror.

"Yes. Here to visit my aunt." William said.

"Oh, that's nice," he said. "Special occasion?"

"Birthday." William said, holding up the card. The cab driver's eyes sharpened.

"You're a good nephew. I'll be lucky if my nephew even sends a text, let alone a card." he complained. The cab slowed down and pulled up outside a nice block of apartments.

"Aunt lives here, eh? Very nice, must be doing something right.

Certainly not driving a cab, that's for sure.

There we go, mate. £14.80 please, bud."

William tapped his card on the pad, wincing. Three seconds later the cabby said, "All done, have a good one!" and the doors unlocked with a clunk.

William stepped out of the cab and onto the street, a bit drier but almost £15 lighter. "Welcome to London." said the cabby out the window as he drove away.

As the cabby turned the corner, he found a place to pull over. He turned his yellow taxi light off, put his badge in the glove compartment, took his signet ring with a black stone out of the ash tray and put it back on his little finger. He called the number.

It rang once then picked up.

"Verification, please?" said a female American voice.

"Yeh, it's *c..a..b, 142, bloodlust 8.*"

"Authenticated. Welcome, brother. How can we be of service today?"

"I have some information." he said.

"I will transfer you now." said the woman. The line rang once more, then a male voice said, "Information, please?"

"It's the Fairchild woman, I think I've found out where she lives. It's the Chiltern Mansions, Old Montague St, White Chapel. Not sure of the flat number, but she has company - her nephew. 5ft 11", medium build, short dark hair, blue eyes. It's her birthday, apparently. That's all."

An automated message now played:

The Blackstones reward loyalty, discard the weak, and destroy the spurious.

Your judgement cometh. There is nothing to fear but fear itself.

Beep.

17

BONDED BY BLOOD

William had found the right block for his aunt's. A brass plaque fixed to the gate said '1 - 4 Chiltern Mansions.'

"She lives at 4, so it must be a penthouse!"

Wow, Aunt Cherri, you are *doing well.*

He climbed up the steps and there was a brass access panel with five buttons on it:

Apartment 4

Apartment 3

Apartment 2

Apartment 1

Concierge 0

He pushed the button for apartment four and it let out a strange warbling tone. He waited. Nothing happened, so he pushed it again.

"Oh no, Aunt Cherri, please don't be out." said William, starting to sit down on the top step.

Just then, a woman's voice said, "Hello, who's there?"

He sprang back up like a jack in the box and said, "Aunt Cherri, it's your nephew, William."

She didn't say anything.

"Hello?"

"Stay right there." she said, in a tone that rooted him to the spot.

A minute later, she was down at the front entrance hall, standing back behind the highly polished glazed door.

"Hi aunt Cherri, it's been-"

"What is your grandfathers name?" she interjected, completely emotionless, her green eyes shining.

"Grampy. I mean, Andrew."

"What painting is in the hallway of his house?"

William drew a blank. "Erm..."

"No erms." scathed Cherri.

"It's a man in military clothing who looks like he needs to sneeze."

She had obviously heard enough. She pushed a button to her left and the door opened inwards into the entrance hall.

It was a grand building.

Very high ceilings, beautiful swirly patterns swept across the tiled floor. It was lit by the most amazing chandelier William had ever seen. The shadows of the crystals created kaleidoscopic shapes on the walls and ceiling. They stepped into a small brass elevator, and Cherri hit the button for the top floor. She didn't say a word. Didn't even look at him.

The elevator stopped and he followed her out onto a landing that led to a large white front door emblazoned with a big, brass number four, smack bang in the centre. There was no lock, just a fingerprint scanner. She put her right thumb onto the black pad, and a little voice said, "ID."

"Cherri - Drinkwater." she said. There were multiple clicks and pops, and the door unbolted itself and opened.

"You can never be too careful." she said.

William followed her inside the apartment. It was like one of those huge Vegas hotel suites where the big spenders get to stay. Everywhere you looked there was marble, brass, glass, and soft furnishings. She walked into the kitchen area and pointed towards a tall stall at the end of the kitchen island. "Sit." she said, like he was a naughty puppy.

And to her, he probably was.

"Tea?" she asked. *Just like Granny would say, but without the 'erm'.*

"Yes, please." William replied.

From what he could tell, there was no place for 'erm' in her life. She seemed like someone who had to be certain of everything and had no time for *dilly dallying,* as his Grampy said sometimes.

"Last time I saw you; you had just finished school." she said.

"What brings you here William?" The kettle was starting to boil.

"Not quite sure where to start, really." he said, as she made the tea.

"At the beginning, preferably." she said, as she handed him his tea in a mug.

William explained about Grampy's accident, which she didn't seem that phased about. Then he told her about the card, the shop and the train ride.

"Has he told you then? Do you know... about London?" she asked.

"Well, he told me a creepy story about a tunnel when he was ten, and the Blackstones." said William.

"His first encounter with the Blackstones." she said. "That still affects him, you know, even after all these years." her green eyes burned into his.

"I saw a few of them today, on the way here." said William. "One of them worked for the underground, and the other was a passenger I bumped into."

Her tone became quite serious. "Were you followed? Did they see where you went?" she demanded.

"I covered my tracks, got out at Moorgate and took a black cab here.

Quite expensive, aren't they?" William said, with a wince.

"Welcome to London." she said, emulating a tour guide.

"Can I have my birthday card, please?"

"Of course." he said, grabbing the card from the inside pocket of his coat and handing it over. "Sorry about the creases." he said timidly.

She took it from him and kneaded out some of them whilst examining the handwriting on the envelope. Then she reached into the centre of the island and picked up a thin silver blade, a letter opener. She made a clean swipe with the blade, opening the card in one go before placing it on the island. She opened the card and didn't seem surprised by the inclusion of newspaper stories. She examined them for a minute before turning them over and placing them onto the island next to the card, like an archaeologist would at the site of a dig. Reading the card now, she nodded before turning to William. He was waiting to see some kind of reaction from the card and its information, but there was nothing.

"I wonder what else your Grampy has told you." she said,

"P.R.S?" she probed.

"Problem, Reaction...Solution." William retorted.

"Very good," she said, smiling like a primary school teacher.

"Triangle of power states?" she shot.

"City of London, Vatican City and erm... erm, Washington DC." he said.

"Excellent, but try and lose the 'erms' William, I have standards." she teased.

"Blackest thing I ever saw?"

"The Blackhouse!" he said, as fast as possible, but she launched her teacup at the wall, and it smashed to smithereens. William froze.

"So, you *did* read my card, then.

Curiosity really did kill the cat you know, William," she hissed.

"What else do you know?" her tone returned to a more stable one.

"Face + hide equals, erm...15808," he said hopefully.

"Wow, you are not as daft as you look, are you William?" she said with an edge. "Missed a bit though, didn't you?"

"How do you mean?" he asked.

"Look at it; It's all there, in the detail." She slid the card over to him and pointed at Grampy's sign off:

SDB 104

Cuthberts Bank.

392 The Strand

London

Something to reflect upon: face + hide.

Love, A.

X

"Is it to do with the bank?" he asked.

"No." she snapped.

"Something to do with the 'Love, A' and kiss?" he asked.

"No." she said, even louder.

"Something to reflect upon... hang on a minute.

Do you have a mirror?" he asked.

"What would you do if you had to improvise?" she said, like a sergeant major.

"Erm."

"No ERMS, William." She shouted.

William's phone was sat on the counter top in front of him, it had turned off and the screen was black. From this angle he could see the chandelier in the lounge reflecting off the black mirror. So, he picked it up and cleaned it a bit with his sleeve. he took out his pad from earlier and placed the phone upright in front so I could see the reflection of the answer he had written: 15808.

To his surprise, the 5 was now a 2.

"12808," he said.

"Well done, William, there's hope for you yet."

She tidied up the bits of broken mug but cut her finger deeply on one of the ceramic shards. She made no fuss, washed it in the sink and wrapped her finger up. She then went to make a few phone calls while William waited in the kitchen. Time was pushing on now, and he thought it was about time for him to leave if he was to get back to Amblefield at a reasonable hour.

Cherri came back into the kitchen and said, "I've spoken to your mum to say where you are, and that you are safe. I told them that you will be home in a day or so."

"What?" said William. "I do have things I need to do, you know; I have a life."

Thoughts of laying in, eating crisps and reading his crap book in the front garden until Jess appeared, flashed before his eyes.

"Well, go back if you must, but I'll be sure to tell your Grampy that you read my card."

"That's blackmail." he said, scornfully.

"Yes, yes, it is, William. Gold star. Soooo proud of you." she said, in her best Granny tone.

My god I hate my family, thought William.

"What do I have to do?" he asked with some reservation.

"Well, things are a bit 'hot' at the moment, shall we say, so I need you to run a little errand for me tomorrow."

"Depends on what it is?" he said.

"I need you to go and fetch that book for me."

"Oh... ok," he said, feeling pleasantly surprised. He thought it was going to be something really boring like one of his mum's favours.

"William, can you go and rake the lawn please?"

"William, can you strip all the wallpaper in the hallway?"

"William, can you pair all these socks please?"

William, William, William... bored, bored, bored.

This was something he could actually do, and probably enjoy for a change.

"I'll be happy to." he said.

"What is the book about?"

"That would be telling, wouldn't it." she said playfully.

"Let's just say it's one of your Grampy's favourite and most precious things in this world, and it should be, as its one of a kind. It's an old book that was made when he was in London. All the secret locations of chambers, tunnels, symbology used by the Blackstones and things to watch out for. Think of it as a survival guide for when the worst happens."

"Things like the tunnel?" he asked.

"Yes, things like that, and much, much worse." she said, in a darker tone.

"So, he fought them, did he...Grampy?" asked William.

"You could say that... When he was strong enough, he and his friends made a stand against some truly dark and twisted people. They almost did it, almost wiped them out entirely, but they spared someone they shouldn't have. Over fifty years have passed, and what started out as a small itch has been left to fester in the dark. Now it's reached into every crack, hole and drain of this city, tainting the memory of the sacrifices they made.

"Now, you can't even turn on the news without the signs being there, taunting us in plain sight. Symbolism in music videos, cartoons, award ceremonies, even football games. Every part of popular culture; Happens so fast sometimes you wouldn't even see it, unless you knew what you were looking for."

"What do you mean?" William asked. "Like the black stone rings?"

"Not just that." she said,

"Symbolism; hand signals.

Here, hand me that remote."

He did so.

She turned on the TV that was hung on the wall next to the fridge. A news channel was on, and the news anchor was talking about an incident that had just happened in New York.

"Watch his hand." she said. "He's going to hand over to another correspondent on location in a second and when he does, pay attention to his hand."

She was right.

"And now, we go over to our New York correspondent Dan McLure." said the news anchor.

He turned to the screen beside him and gave a wave to Dan in New York, but his hand was more like the kind of thing you'd see at a rock concert. Devil horns. Very fast, but it happened. There was the usual two second delay, then

Dan said, "Thanks Greg." and put his right hand inside his coat enough to hide his hand. Aunt Cherri muted the TV.

"See that?" she asked, holding her hand out with the devil horns. "See this?" She placed her hand in her cardigan. "It's a greeting. Basically saying, 'I'm a member, are you?'"

Waving her devil horns.

Then she placed her hand inside her cardigan.

'Yes... I... am.'"

William was shocked. *Was it really that out in the open? Were these people really everywhere?*

"There are those of us that fight, but it has to be kept secret, as they are everywhere.

The information in that book will turn the tide in the favour of either side that gets it. They know it exists; they just don't know where. They are always watching me, so you must get the book. Can I rely on you?" she asked, exactly like Grampy.

18

HAVE A BANANA

▼

William woke up early as the light was pouring in through the windows of the penthouse. Looking out over Whitechapel, the rays of sunlight bounced off the glass of the buildings opposite and onto the cars, lighting up the road in long oval spots. London was just waking up, and so was he.

He wandered through the corridor and into the kitchen area to get a drink. His aunt Cherri was already up, dressed, and looked ready for the day ahead. A kettle boiled next to her, and she was already making him a mug of tea.

"Thanks." he said, taking the same stool as the night before. She placed the tea in front of him and started to make breakfast.

"What's the best way to get to The Strand, then?" asked William, taking a sip.

"Aldgate East. Circle and district line, six stops west." she said, without hesitation.

"Wow, you could work for the Underground." he said cheekily.

"I like to keep my head above ground, thank you. Much safer that way." she said as she started to unload the dishwasher. William noticed that the cut on her hand had pretty much gone already.

"The cut on your finger." said William,

"What about it?" she asked, realising what he meant.

"It's healed up. How can something that bled that much be healed already?" asked William.

"Some cuts aren't as deep as they look, William."

They finished breakfast and William asked if he could take a shower.

"Yes, of course," she said. "In the room you slept in, there's a wardrobe with some clothes in it. You are bound to find something that will fit you in there."

Why did she have men's clothing? He wondered.

The previous night, William had seen quite a few photos in silver frames, but the thing was, they were all destinations.

Beautiful sunsets over cliffs, the Great Wall of China (he had recognised it from geography), lakes, rivers, deserts, mountains, but no people. *Why were there no people?* He thought of this while he showered.

The truth was that there had been men around, but never for long. Cherri had always found it difficult to let people in.

By day, she ran a very successful business importing antiquities from around the world. But her real interest, her passion in life, was carrying on the work started by Andrew. And she was bloody good at it, even if she did say so herself.

Once showered, he dried himself off and headed back to the room that he had slept in. Sure enough, the wardrobe did have all manner of men's clothes inside. He picked out a pair of dark blue jeans and a T-shirt with Pink Floyd's 'Dark Side of the Moon' artwork on it. It shows a triangular prism effect, with white light hitting one side, being split into multiple colours. It kind of felt a fitting symbol for today. On the outside, we may all look the same, but underneath we could be completely different colours. He grabbed a red baseball cap too.

They walked out of the penthouse and the large white door closed behind them. Multiple locks snapped and popped into place as they walked towards the elevator.

Cherri started barking orders.

"Don't talk to anyone; Don't look at anyone; Don't even breathe that loudly. You know that nasal thing you used to do when you were six? Ahh, it was so annoying."

They walked into the elevator. The barrage of orders continued. They stepped out of the elevator on the ground floor.

"Don't deviate from the route we talked about and don't draw attention to yourself. Stay safe! And if in doubt-"

"Run?" William said hopefully.

"Don't. If in doubt, don't! Just don't, ok?! Understand? I will wait for you at the coffee shop in Somerset House. Two hours, William, two hours."

It was 10:30 AM. He walked out of the lobby and down the stairs into the street. He decided to walk to the station and save some money, plus it was a nice day, and in London that's not something to pass up.

He weaved through the back streets watching his phone for the directions to Aldgate East. Only a ten-minute walk. *Probably do it in eight,* he thought. So many parked cars here.

Why isn't everyone at work?

Then it dawned on him. They probably were, but went in by the Tube like everyone else.

William walked out onto Whitechapel High Street and saw Aldgate East station in the distance, feeling the tension building inside him already, just from the idea of having to go back on the Tube. He tapped through and followed the signs for circle and district, west. He had missed the Monday morning rush, so the platforms were pretty much empty, which was a relief.

A tube pulled in and he boarded it right near the front, and as there were so many free seats, he took one. As they pulled off, he thought of the conversation he had with his aunt about Grampy fighting these horrible people and wondered how serious it had actually got.

His grampy was a big man, even now, and had a grip of steel. William once saw him lose his temper with a lawn mower that had refused to start. He picked it up, bent it in half, and threw it over the fence into the next door's garden. He dreaded to think the kind of damage he could have done when he was younger.

The journey round to Temple was smooth. A few people got on and off, but no Blackstones, no weird hand gestures and nobody eating babies' fingers like they were chicken nuggets.

He stepped out onto the platform at Temple and followed the yellow signs to the exit, only to find no escalator.

"Ahhh, bloody stairs!" he sighed. "Come on, William...don't, William," he said to himself as he started to climb them.

'If in doubt, don't.' aunt Cherri had said.

Well, I'm having doubts about these stairs, that's for sure.

Once at the top, he took a moment to catch his breath and headed towards the barriers to tap out. Once he was back out on the street, the cool air helped ease his chest a bit. He crossed the road so he could walk by the river.

Such an important part of London, the Thames. After all, It's why the Romans chose the settlement. The water was quite calm, and the sun was highlighting the peaks as it shimmered. All the tour boats and river ferries were full, and megaphones could be heard over the road noise explaining what landmarks lie ahead.

"And coming up on our right, we have the Egyptian Obelisk, Cleopatra's Needle." said a tour guide from the nearest riverboat.

William walked under the Kingsway tunnel bridge and could see the very top of the Obelisk just above the trees ahead. Getting it there all those years ago must have been quite a task.

Nerdy fact alert: Cleopatra's Needle

It was originally gifted to Britain in 1819 by Muhammed Ali Pasha, ruler of Egypt, but it had nothing to do with Cleopatra. That was actually the name of the ship that was specifically designed to transport it to London, but names have a habit of sticking.

Because of how large and heavy it is, the cost of shipping it to Britain was considered to too high by the prime minister, Lord Liverpool. So, it stayed in Alexandria until 1877, until the funding for transportation was provided by an English surgeon and dermatologist called Sir Erasmus Wilson.

Although he was not actually knighted until 1881.

This generous contribution to London probably played a big part in his social status upgrade.

The transportation costs were north of £10,000, which in today's money is more than a million. A special iron casing had to be made and shipped to Alexandria, along with all the guide ropes, pulleys, and other lifting equipment. Once the Obelisk was secured on board, they made their journey back carefully. Disaster almost struck in the Bay of Biscay (large indentation of sea between France and Spain) and the boat had to be rescued. Six people sadly lost their lives. The Needle finally reached the Thames on January 21st 1878 but wasn't erected until September 12th that year. It has a sister needle that is erected in Central Park, New York.

• • • ● • ● • • •

William thought of Grampy's lecture about the triangle of power and the three states. It had just occurred to him that all three had a monolith, an Obelisk like structure in close proximity.

The Vatican City had the Caligula's Obelisk, another Egyptian one, right in the middle of St Peter's Square. Washington DC has the Washington monument. Although it's modern compared to the others, at 169 meters tall, it is by far the largest. And finally, in London, there was the needle. William was starting to see a pattern emerging, but now wasn't the time to get side-tracked.

He checked his map and took a right up Savoy Street. Quite a strange road on an incline, with a garden to one side. According to his map, The Strand was just up at the top of the road, so he was close. Once at the top, he crossed the road and looked for no 392.

Found it!

It was a quirky place. A modern building that was made to look old.

Having some heritage in London is the key to reassuring people, especially when it comes to money.

William saw there was a push button outside the door. This was no ordinary bank, and it was quite posh.

"That's it, William...that's it." he said to himself, trying to steady his nerves.

He pushed the button and waited.

19

Just So…

"Good morning, Cuthbert's Bank." said a surly lady over the intercom.

"Erm, good morning." said William, nervously into the box. "I have a safety deposit box here."

"No problem, Sir." said the woman, "Jake will be out to tend to your needs at once."

"Thank you." he said, but she had already gone.

Good old Jake, eh. Where do they find these people?

With Williams own future hanging in the balance, he often wondered how these people find these jobs. Right families? Right friends? Do you think that this 'Jake', whoever the hell he is, woke up one day and thought, *you know what, Mother, I'd like to work in a posh bank and leave people freezing their bum off on the street because I can't be bothered to...*

"Hello, Sir, my name is Jake. How can I help you today?" William turned around to face the soft voice. He was large man. Really large, like a wrestler. William didn't think they could actually make a suit that big, yet Jake spoke with the most eloquent voice, and William heard each and every syllable.

"I have a safety deposit box here and I'd like to take something out, please." said William.

"No problem, Sir, please follow me."

They walked into the bank, but it didn't really look like a bank at all. More like a five-star hotel lobby. Each side of the main area was lined with freestanding fabric-covered dividers that created adaptable meeting areas, with client discretion in mind. Some light piano music could be heard over the hidden speakers; Not too loud, not too quiet, just so.

He led William over to an area that was free and asked him to take a seat, so he did. The chair was an old green leather type and was very comfortable. After all the stairs at Temple station, his legs needed a break. Jake arranged the dividers to provide him with some privacy.

"Can I get you anything to drink, Sir? Some tea perhaps?" asked Jake.

"That would be lovely." said William, never feeling more common in his life. As soon as Jake had walked away, he was replaced by a smartly dressed woman in her fifties who introduced herself as Octavia, holding a small pad and pen, both emblazoned with the gilded banks logo.

"Safety deposit box number and surname please." she asked, warmly.

"Sure, it's *SDB 104* and the surname is Fairchild." he said, without having to check his notes for once.

"Thank you." she said, and as she moved back towards her desk she was immediately replaced with Jake, holding a silver tray of tea paraphernalia. He placed the tray down with the lightest touch and served the tea like a waiter. Such a strange experience, considering he was supposed to be in a bank.

Williams bank, back in Perinsgrove, looked more like a prison reception-come-post office in comparison. Dirty Perspex everywhere with little microphones that cut in and out at the most crucial parts of instructions, howling with feedback occasionally. This made whoever was at the front wince, while long lines of people waited inpatiently for the one position that's serving out of eight.

Having to watch pale, sweaty bank workers behind the other screens chat amongst themselves, remarking on how busy it is.

Like a social experiment on how to enrage people.

Jake had finished serving the tea and said, "If there is anything else you need, please just raise your hand and I will come right over."

"Thank you very much, Jake."

"You are welcome, Sir." he said.

William had a thought. *I tell you what, if I actually finish uni and find a job that's worth having, I'm going to bank with these people. It's brilliant.*

Before too long Octavia was back. This time she had a man beside her, holding a metal box with flashing lights and technology bolted to it.

"Hello, Sir, SDB104 is here." she said, ushering the man to set it down on the table in front of William. He did so, again, with the lightest touch. This was it. It was about the size of an A3 paper box that stationers sell, only polished metal. On the side facing William was a brass tag riveted to the box that said "104", and a small touch screen device that had a digitized version of the bank's logo spinning slowly in the centre.

He reached out and touched the screen once. A small voice emitted from the device, and politely asked for the account surname. At the same time, two hands in white leather gloves had appeared on screen also, they were signing what the little man was saying. Kind of like playing a game of charades with Mickey Mouse, without the body.

"Fairchild." he said.

"Account surname not recognised, please try again." the machine said. The white gloved hands more animated now.

William panicked.

What? Was this going to be a waste of time after all? Would they even let me finish my tea before Jake picked me up and carried me out onto the cold street, only to place me on my head on the pavement, oh so gently?

He tried again.

"Fair-Child." he said, louder and clearer, reminding him of how his dad spoke when they went to Spain.

"Accepted." said the little man in the box, as the white gloved hand gave two thumbs up.

The bank logo stopped spinning and turned from gold to green, but the green soon wore off.

The logo shrank and moved up to the top of the screen and started to rotate again. Five blank spaces appeared underneath like a game of hangman, and a keypad with the numbers 0 to 9, a backspace, and a confirm button. William felt his heart beating fiercely in his chest, so he had a sip of his tea.

Breathe, William, just breathe.

His hands were shaking, so he pulled them into fists a few times. That seemed to help. He knew the number; Aunt Cherri had made him memorise it over and over in the lift.

1...5...8...0...8

No, no, no... hang on. *Something to reflect upon and remember.* The five was now a two. So, he hit the backspace and went again.

1...2...8...0...8

He placed his finger over the confirm button and closed his eyes before letting his finger seal his fate. As he pushed the button he opened his eyes. The screen went foggy, and a loading wheel appeared in the centre. It seemed to take forever, and he felt paranoid that all the staff were listening in on him. Suddenly the screen went back to the golden spinning logo.

Oh my god, must have been the wrong number. Why, why...

Just then, the logo turned green, and the box clicked. It was open.

William stood up so he could take the lid off. The metal lid was quite heavy as it had all the mechanisms built in. He placed it on the table next to the box on its rubber seal. He looked inside the box and was surprised to see a cloth bag. He reached in and picked the bag up and looked inside at the bulging red book. It was very old, about the size of a diary, and the spine was starting to fray at the ends. The front cover was plain except for a small drawing of a single lit candle in the top left-hand corner.

'*Do not* read the book in the bank.' he heard his aunt Cherri's words ring in his ears, making him recoil like it was bank teller feedback.

Ok, ok, he thought, putting the book in the inside pocket of his coat. He placed the lid back on the deposit box and sat down.

A message had appeared on the screen, this time it read, 'Secure box?' with a 'Yes' and 'No' button alongside it. He pressed the 'Yes' button and the box made a series of clicks to indicate it was locked. The message on the screen said, 'Goodbye' and the little white hands waved before fading into black. William raised his hand, and Jake walked straight over as promised.

"Hello, Sir, how can I be of service?" he said evenly.

"I've finished with my box now and would like to return it please." he said happily.

"Certainly, Sir." he said, and he raised his right hand, pointed to the ceiling and clicked once.

The man who had dropped the box off, was there in an instant to collect it and he did so without any sound. Another man came in immediately after and wiped the table down, ensuring it returned to its high state of shine before leaving.

"Is there anything else I can do for you today, Sir?" asked Jake.

"I'd like to leave now, please." William said, half expecting the worst, like a bill for the tea.

"Of course, Sir." He moved one of the dividers and William stood up. Just as when they came in, he led him to the front door, opened it ahead of him, and bowed slightly as William walked through.

"Have a good day, Sir." he said.

"And you Jake, and you." said William, looking back.

20

EYES ON THE PRIZE

William walked out into The Strand like he'd just won the lottery. Such great service. He checked his map and walked east towards Somerset House, hoping the coffee shop was easy to find. As he walked along the main road, he heard the squeal of tyres behind him, someone was in a rush. Just then, out of nowhere, a black van mounted the pavement in front of him and slammed on its brakes, blocking his path.

A man with sunglasses jumped out.

William panicked. He did what he wasn't supposed to do and ran. My god, did he run. As he ran, he could feel the diary slapping him on the chest from his coat pocket. He ran left, up Exeter St, and sprinted around the bend, just catching sight of another black van pulling in. It was a one-way street, but these people, whoever they were, had no respect for road etiquette. William's legs were really burning now, and the baseball cap had slipped off under a car. Just as he got to Burleigh Street, he saw another black van enter the street ahead. He turned left and sprinted off up towards Tavistock Street.

He tripped on a manhole on Tavistock Street and almost got hit by a car coming down. It slammed on its brakes, and he slid over the bonnet slightly. William carried on running until he couldn't run anymore and ended up by the Aldwych theatre, panting and bent double trying to catch his breath.

Lost them, he thought, as his heart rate started to slow.

He walked back down the main road past all the hotels and small theatres whose bright lights brought this part of the city to life in the evening, flinching every time a car revved too hard or backfired. Crossing roads in London is dangerous and it's not necessarily the cars you have to be wary of. It's the cyclists, who are better known as silent assassins. They move very quickly, rarely stop for red lights, and you can't hear them coming. He crossed the road at a main intersection that had the strangest building; the front of it was curved. he should have been paying more attention though, as a cyclist almost ran straight into him.

"Oi, watch where you're going you bloody idiot." said the cyclist whose anger rolled away as quickly as he did.

William made it across the junction, just, and he was almost back where he started, doubling back on himself, and twenty meters up ahead of him was the back of Somerset House.

He crossed the road again and both black vans pulled up in a hurry, screeching to a stop.

"I don't believe it." he said to himself, as he started to run again.

They must really want this book.

He pounded through the arches and into Somerset House, under the covered section in the courtyard, and he could hear the clatter of footsteps chasing him on the pavement behind him. Seeking out signs for the coffee shop, he saw a logo of a cup on the right.

That's it.

He sprinted into the building.

His aunt Cherri must have heard the commotion as he could see her standing by a service door. She was waving her hand, willing him to hurry up. The door was propped open by someone in a flak jacket, and William could see a couple of other people in the corridor. William reached into his coat pocket and pulled out the red journal, holding it out in front like a baton in a relay race. Her green eyes danced.

"I got it...I got it." said William, trying to catch his breath whilst handing it over.

"Sorry, William, don't tell them anything, ok?" said Cherri, before taking the book and hitting him so hard in the temple with it, that he blacked out.

21

LEFT FOR DEAD

William woke up to confusion and a dull headache. The only light he could see was a tiny lamp inside the back of the van.

They have me. I am done for, he thought.

He could hear the radio playing a song from behind the bulkhead. *'Do you like pina coladas... and getting caught in the rain...'*

The man sat opposite him was wearing all black, sunglasses, and had a Blackstone ring on.

Of course, he did. It didn't surprise William that Satanists had terrible taste in music either. Not one bit.

"Where are you taking me?" he asked, feeling quite weary.

"Shut up." said the man opposite, forcefully. "You will see for yourself."

William felt the van veer left and then go down like they were going under a tunnel. The stretch of road lasted for ages; down and down they went, then a right turn at the end. The van slowed and soon came to a stop. He heard the terrible music stop and the front doors of the van open and shut. Footsteps made their way round to the back of the van and both doors opened at once, with two men dressed in black, one on either side, each with little signet rings.

"You guys really should try a bit harder with the outfits, you know. They look a bit... tired." said William.

"Get up," said the man opposite, as he manhandled him out of the van into the grips of the other two.

"Is it like working at a restaurant? You start off with no Blackstone and get more as you go along? Or is it more like the scouts?" William teased, knowing full well they wouldn't answer.

They dragged him through what looked to be a giant underground car park with no windows. Just bright lighting and huge fans bringing in fresh air from above. They took him to a room at the far side.

"Should have parked a bit closer." said William.

SMACK. One of the guards punched him right in the ear, and it howled.

"Owww!"

"Not so funny now, is it?" said the guard. He locked him into a pair of silver handcuffs that were suspended from the concrete ceiling by a thick chain.

"Enjoy your stay." said the other one, emulating a hotel concierge, just before punching him hard in the stomach. They both laughed as they shut the door behind them.

Here he was, in a small concrete box room, God only knows how deep underground, handcuffed with his arms above his head.

No chair, couldn't even sit down if there was one.

He'd finished coughing his guts up when another man walked in. The room went cold.

He was a tall man, clean shaven with piercing blue eyes and an expression that looked like he had just been charged too much for something. And right now, William was the shopkeeper. He decided to play dumb.

"What is your name?" he asked, in a European accent. William's ear was still ringing from the punch.

"William Fairchild."

"Ahh, another Fairchild, I see." he said, in a tone of an angry headmaster having to deal with a well-known troublemaker's new sibling.

"Your Aunt is well known to us; you are quite the prize catch.

Where is the book?" he asked coldly.

"She has it." said William, gesturing to the lump on the side of his head.

"Ouch." he said. "Been a naughty boy, have we, huh?"

"No, I think it was an accident" said William, but he knew it wasn't. She did this on purpose. Although he still didn't understand why.

'Sorry, William, don't tell them anything, OK?' BANG. *The memory repeated.*

"You obviously do not know your aunt very well. She doesn't make mistakes. We have lost hundreds of members because of her and her team. She either kills them or turns them against us. Simple as that.

So where do you fit in with all of this, I wonder?" pondered Cameron.

"I don't know what you are talking about. It was just a book; An art book. My aunt deals in antiques, she's not involved in anything like that. You must have the wrong person," said William.

"Really? So, what about Andrew Fairchild?" He looked on, willing William to give him some kind of reaction. "I guess that would make you his... grandson?" he pried.

"Died last year; Cancer." William said, dryly. "Never really knew him anyway."

"Interesting!...Thank you ever so much, I was not aware." he said, practically salivating. "Let's cut to the chase, shall we?"

"No more please, I've run all day and my legs are killing me." William uttered.

"Funny boy, I see.

You have just one chance of getting out of this alive.

We are going to get your aunt on the phone and arrange a trade.

You... for the book. If she won't do the deal, then you my boy, will never see daylight again. Understood?" he threatened.

William had a chance at least. Aunt Cherri would set up the trade, make a double cross, get him back and they'd be sitting around her kitchen island with a mug of tea, reading that book and maybe eating that pizza he saw at the back of her fridge... unless it was Hawaiian.

Who had the idea of putting pineapple on pizza? It's a disgrace.

The man took out his phone and dialled. "Yes, it's *Darkone 14... yum, yum, baby*.

Please use the database, and connect me to Cherri Fairchild's mobile.

Yes, I'm aware it's untraceable. It always has been, just put me through."

The line rang and he put his phone on speakerphone. The call connected.

"I was starting to think you would never call, Cameron," said Cherri.

"I have something that belongs to you, or should I say, someone," he said.

"Prove it." said Cherri.

Cameron reached out and pressed his thumb onto the bump on William's head incredibly hard.

"AGHHHHHH." William shouted,

"Aunt Cherri, It's William. They think your involved in-"

CRUNCH.

Cameron kicked him squarely in the nether regions. He crumpled up, looking like a chicken in the butcher's window, hanging from the rail.

"Heard that one." Cherri said. "Oh yes, you do by the sounds of it. What's the matter, Cameron, do you not want him anymore?" she teased.

"Well, he's fun but I'd prefer something to read."

"There are plenty of libraries in London." she poked.

"Let's cut the crap, shall we? You know how this works; I'm only going to ask you once:

The boy for the book."

William felt sick, probably from being kicked in his special area, but there was something else. The adrenaline of waiting for someone to pull a trigger, or a race just about to start.

His heart was in his mouth and the silence was deafening.

"The book is mine, Cameron; Kill him if you must." she said, then the line went dead.

William was stunned. Absolutely floored that his own aunt would sell him down the river to some crackpot Satanists for a poxy book with maps. A bloody book. His life is worth less than a book. He gave up and hung from the chains for a bit. The handcuffs were cutting into his wrists, but he didn't care anymore.

"See what I mean, boy? Absolutely ruthless." said Cameron.

William nodded from his dressed chicken pose. "Can you get on with it then?" he asked. "You know, killing me?"

Cameron laughed hysterically.

"No, boy, I have a plan for you. A very special day approaches: Tomorrow night you will be a part of the Blackmass.

I can't wait to see the look on the members' faces when they know we'll be sacrificing a Fairchild. I'm so happy." He jiggled on the spot a bit before catching himself.

"So, I have to keep you alive... for now." With that, he hit a button by the door that dropped the suspended chain. William lay in a heap on the floor underneath it.

22

AS ABOVE, SO BELOW

William must have passed out because he woke to a man entering the room while he was still crumpled on the floor. He too had a Blackstone ring, just like all the others, but he also had a tattoo on his face. Up at the edge of his eye was a single black tear. He had a large plastic bottle of water with him and a sandwich. He placed the items next to William and sat on the floor in front of the door, blocking any chance of exit.

"Eat." he said. "You'll need it."

William was starving as he hadn't eaten since breakfast. All the running and being beaten up had used all of his reserves, so much so that he felt a bit shaky. He was so hungry, in fact, that his usual disdain for tomatoes was completely forgotten.

"Not that bad." he said, in between bites and breaths. When he finished the sandwich, he checked the packet for a rogue bit of cheese, feeling quite disappointed that he didn't find one.

"So, how did you get into this?" William asked, "you know, Satan and all that stuff?"

The man looked back at him with emotionless eyes and just when William thought he was going to tell him to 'shut up' or try and punch him, he simply sighed.

"Why do you care?" he asked.

"I've just found out that I'm going to be sacrificed," said William.

"Blackmass" said the Blackstone.

"They have been after you Fairchilds for a long time."

"I can't see what good killing me will do." said William, starting to feel the weight of it all.

"It's not about the good, it's about change." said the Blackstone.

"Change?" William pried.

The man took a deep breath.

"Growing up, my mother was always sick. Always something going on at the hospital. We were a Christian family, and I prayed every day. I mean, every day.

I prayed for my mum to get better; I prayed for my dad to stop drinking, find a job and keep it."

"I hear you." said William.

The man continued...

"I prayed that I'd get the chance to better myself, and that the country would wake up one day and see what we were doing to each other.

But I never heard God's voice, and it didn't work. My mum just got sicker and sicker until the day she died. I was so angry. My dad lost his mind and would beat me black and blue. He got to a point where he couldn't take it anymore and ended up throwing himself in front of a Monday morning train."

"That's terrible." said William, "What did you do then?"

"Thirteen years old and on my own, I fell in with some rough people and ended up getting to know a guy who was part of what he called 'The Blackstones'.

He vouched for me, and I joined. It was small stuff at first, but they always made sure I ate and had somewhere to sleep, and for the first time I felt like I was a part of something.

"As time went on, I had to do more. It's a pyramid, you see.

You have to put the work in to get anything out. The first time I saw a dark magic ritual I was like, 'this stuff isn't for real,' but it was. It worked. They achieved something that was otherwise impossible, and that's more than *he* ever did for me." he said, looking up.

"What about your soul?" William asked.

"What about it?" he said.

"If this is how God treats some people on earth, I don't want to set foot in their kingdom."

William sipped the water and couldn't argue with him. If he had been dealt those cards, would he have felt the same? Seems like being the king of all that is good isn't enough sometimes. A bit of intervention would go a long way.

The day rolled on and when the time had come, they forced him out of the room, down a corridor and into a shower. When he got out, his clothes were missing, but there was a white robe on the dressing table that he had to wear. Before long he was being dragged back through the carpark, like a spa guest getting thrown out for weeing in the sauna, and stuffed into the back of the same black van they arrived in.

A different man was now in the back with William, and he had no interest in talking. He just reached forward to tie a blindfold around his bruised head. William could feel the van move. They travelled for around ten minutes but stayed low. It didn't feel like they had come up at all. Sub-terranean London is so deep. So many tunnels and hidden parts in the city.

The van stopped again, and he was dragged out into another corridor. William was starting to feel nervous and could hear sinister music being played on massive speakers, and a general hubbub of people, almost like being at a theatre or cinema. He was escorted through another set of doors and into a small holding room at the side of what seemed to be a stage area. William was handcuffed to the table, sat down, and had his blindfold removed.

The men left him there and shut the door. It was a grey box with no windows, like a dark police interrogation room, but he could hear what was going on.

"Brothers and sisters." he heard the distinctive voice of Cameron say, his voice booming through the speakers. The crowd calmed down and were soon silent.

"Brothers and sisters, welcome to our 40th Blackmass. This year we are at the Prima chiesa, St P's."

"St P's?" said William. "This is happening at St Paul's? What the actual..."

"First things first: housekeeping." said Cameron. "Please ensure you wear your robes correctly at all times, so we don't know who you are. Just in case you haven't been here before, toilets are located in the lobby, but try and hold on for the interval if you can.

Fire exits are located by the running man symbols, but please, in the event of a fire, don't run."

A small chuckle came from the crowd.

"We have one hell of a Blackmass lined up for you tonight, so give it up for your supreme overlord, Keeper of the Darkhearts, the one, the only... Jacob!"

There was an eruption of applause from the audience that lasted for ages, and then it just stopped, instantly, like someone turned the sound off.

Boom... Boom... Boom...

"Light and shade." Jacob bellowed. "Good and evil, right and wrong, up and down. It's all the same, depending on your perspective." William could hear footsteps on the stage.

"*They* live their lives in the light, whilst *we* are forced to work in the shadows. They are the Good, we are the Evil. They do what they want, and *we* take all the blame. Well, no more!" Applause rippled through the stands.

"Even now, our pieces move slowly into position. Every government, every corporation, foundation, trust, and organisation. We plan to have one in all. And many are here today." More applause rippled.

"They are so caught up with protecting themselves they failed to notice the King. For He is open, unguarded. The dark age of our domination is almost at hand. The planets move closer every day and when the time is right, he shall return.

Real change is coming - are you with me?"

The crowd roared.

"Hail, Satan."

"Hail, Satan."

"Hail, Satan."

The crowd sounded like a football match, or a war chant. William had never heard such a tribe.

"Hail, Satan."

"Hail, Satan."

Boom....Boom...Boom,

The room fell silent.

"Tonight, we tell the tale of not one lost sheep, but two.

The young shepherd worked hard in the summer months when the weather was pleasant. He tended to his flock and made sure they were fed and watered. He kept them safe and often camped out. But towards the end of the autumn, the young shepherd didn't find the colder weather appealing, so he started to stay in his hut more often than he used to. The sheep were scared, but slowly got used to his absence.

By the time winter had arrived, the shepherd hardly left his hut at all as it was too cold for him. He had forgotten about the wolves. The wolves were hungry now, as they too had been outside in all weather. They watched the flock in the distance and observed how the sheep were not tended to. Some of the sheep were bored of their surroundings and had eaten all the grass they could find. They hungered for greener pasture, which caused them to wander."

William heard more footsteps on the stage, followed by the sound of empty cups on stoneware. The crowd clapped.

"The wandering lamb didn't even know what wolves were. All they were interested in was the grass that grew further and further away from the shepherd's hut. The wolves watched, and they waited…"

More footsteps and the grating noise of a knife being sharpened.

"When the time was right, the wolves attacked."

A man let out a mighty roar, and the crowd cheered.

What on earth are they doing? Is it a play? wondered William, muttering to himself from his room, just off stage.

He could now hear the chinking of cups, like a toast of some sort.

Boom... Boom... Boom...

The room settled down and the crowd became quiet again.

"Another young sheep grew tired of being tethered to a gate." Jacob boomed. "His owner was out hunting for wolves."

"BOOO", some of the crowd jeered.

"The hunter stayed out too long and forgot about the lonely young sheep they had tied up, and the wolves walked slowly and confidently towards their next meal."

Just then, three large men in black robes came into the room and unlocked William's handcuffs. They frog marched him out into the bright lights of the theatre stage. The warmth of the lights gave him a brief sense of relief, until he heard the laughter of the huge audience, which was in the thousands.

As his eyes adjusted, he could now see a large blood-stained white marble altar in front of him. It had carved leaves at the edges that were still dripping with blood. A fierce character with that massive voice stood in the centre of the stage with a staff in hand. He was an older man and had an angular face with defined features. He was dressed in a long black cape with gold embroidery and Blackstones, sewn in.

*This can't be happening. Cherri must be here, she must...*thought William, desperately trying to make out a familiar face or eyes.

Jacob continued, "This particular sheep was the prized possession of the hunter, and its kin had been in the hunter's family for centuries. I present to you... a Fairchild!"

The crowd went ballistic, and the stamping of their feet sounded like thunder. William struggled to free himself from their grips, but they were too strong. They lifted William up onto the already bloodied altar and laid him down. As they tied his hands and feet, more China cups were placed on their marks under the marble leaves at the edges. The crowd had become so quiet with anticipation you could hear every movement. Jacob continued...

"Knowing the hunter had abandoned the young sheep, the wolves moved in..."

William heard the footsteps enter from side of the stage and come closer to him, until the figure stood above him. The face that looked down from the darkened robe was that of Cameron. William had given up trying to free himself and could feel the hot tears of desperation running down his face and into his ears, muffling the sounds of the audience's murmuring, encouraged by the excitement and anticipation. He saw the silver dagger as it reflected off the stage lights and into his eyes. *This is it, it's over.*

He thought of his mother sitting out in the garden in the sun. Then of Jess and her beautifully curled hair, lovely brown eyes, and cute smile. He even thought of Granny and her "erms" but the strongest thought of all was his Grampy. Looking up at Cameron, the dagger was now high above his head.

The sound of the room muted down. William heard his grampy's voice in his head,

OK, Bill, shhh... shhh. It's ok, my boy, just breathe.

He closed his eyes and slowly exhaled, waiting to feel the strike of the blade, but heard an "ooof" instead. The room fell silent.

William opened his eyes and felt the hot blood trickling down on his face from above.

Cameron was still holding the dagger above his head but had an arrow sticking out of his throat. He gurgled, dropped the dagger, and fell backwards, clenching his neck. The dagger clattered on the floor.

Screams came over from the direction of the crowd, and it was like two thousand people jumped up and tried to leave at the same time. More arrows were ricocheting off the marble architecture and finding themselves embedded in woodwork. A black robed member started to untie the ropes that bound William to the altar, and he sat up as soon as he could, wiping the tears and blood away from his face. The member pulled back their hood to reveal that it was his aunt Cherri, her green eyes looking at him intently when she said,

"I can explain everything, but we need to go, now!"

The fight continued. Many fighters who were also in black robes were shooting crossbows down from the gallery seats, and some were fighting hand to hand with others. It was almost impossible to tell who anyone was except the soldiers who had their hoods down, and you could see their faces. Just then a man was thrown from the balcony with a cry and hit the floor right by the front row.

"Come on...this way," said Cherri.

They ran up the theatre steps until they saw the exit signs for the lobby. Out in the lobby, more chaos ensued with people being thrown into cabinets and vending machines, scattering shards of broken glass and confectionery all over the black & white checked floor. A trail of black robes had been discarded on the floor and the people were scrambling to get onto minibuses parked outside in the underground carpark. You could see the bloodstains on their clothing, and some were limping. One man who had taken an arrow to the leg was left behind by two others. He lay on the cold concrete of the carpark with outstretched arms, willing them to return. Some of the buses were already full and were driving off in a hurry. The passengers ducking down as much as possible to avoid being seen.

Cherri pointed to a car that was waiting for them at the end of the level. They ran to it and a soldier stepped out, saying, "Ma'am." On his flak jacket there was an embroidered logo: the same single lit candle that was in the case and on the book.

"Jacob is here!" said Cherri. "I want him alive." The soldier nodded and sprinted inside, removing a machete from his belt as he ran.

They got in the car and Cherri drove across the car park with the tires screeching on the dry concrete. The ramps just kept going up and up. William had lost count at eight. By the time he could see the final exit, he was starting to feel a bit sick.

The car smashed through the checkered exit barrier, and it broke off as the car leapt out onto the street. Suddenly, they were on a roundabout. William looked behind them and was surprised to see a high-rise office block with an underground carpark.

23

Clarity

William didn't speak for about an hour on the way back to Amblefield. He was too angry and his hand had developed a tremor that he couldn't shake away. Cherri had decided it was best if she took him back to his grandparents' tonight, just in case.

They were getting close to Amblefield when Cherri said, "William, speak to me. are you OK?"

"What do you think?" he said, angrily, feeling the rage building inside him.

"You make me go and collect a book, then I get chased by these nutters in black vans.

I managed to do what you asked me to do and met you at Somerset House. Then, you knocked me out with the book and let these vile creatures take me down into the depths of wherever the hell we were?

They beat the living crap out of me!

And when that weird Cameron guy called you to make a deal, *you* told him to KILL ME!"

"I can see why y-" she began.

"Then...I'm transported again to another underground bunker and locked in another dark room. Only to be dragged on stage and almost sacrificed in front of thousands of people dressed in black robes. HOW DO YOU THINK I AM? HUH?" William fumed.

"I know, I know, William. It seems harsh what I did to you, but it had to be this way. The book provided me with the precise locations of all the underground chambers, including the one under St Paul's. We had found out a few weeks ago that the Blackmass was going ahead at what they called the 'prima chiesa' or 'first church', but we didn't know where it was until we had the book, thanks to you.

I knew that they wouldn't have just killed a Fairchild, as they have been after us for decades."

William remembered what he had told them. "I told Cameron that Grampy had died, and that I didn't really know him."

"Good job!" she said, looking shocked. "I've spent so long worrying about him. It's a relief if they think he's dead already. Why didn't I think of that?"

"Anyway...I knew they would have to include you in the ceremony, as the Blackstones would love it. Nobody would want to miss it either, which meant the security would be more lax than normal, providing the perfect distraction for us to strike."

"You used me as bait!? Your own family!... Unbelievable." said William, angrily.

"There was no other way. William, I am truly sorry you thought I'd thrown you to the sharks. That would never happen, never.

These people are usually unpredictable, cold and calculating. Having the upper hand is a rare opportunity that we could not pass up."

"And you knew you could rescue me?" William asked.

"Nothing in life is for certain, William, nothing.

But my men are some of the finest in their field. The one who got Cameron is my captain and I trust him with my life, and tonight, yours too."

"It was a good shot." he said, taking a moment.

"So, what about this Jacob? Will you get him?"

"I don't know, I'll find out tomorrow." she said worriedly. "On that note, keep an eye on the news. You'll see quite a few celebrities or public figures will have either died of mysterious causes, or have just simply disappeared tomorrow."

"I'm sure Grampy will have his work cut out. He'll probably send you a card or two," said William.

"Yes, he does like a card." She drove on, putting the radio on in the search for news.

They pulled into the drive at Granny and Grampy's around midnight and some of the lights were still on.

"Are you coming in?" William asked.

"I can't; I have a lot of mess to clear up tomorrow, as you can probably tell."

"Be careful driving back; It's a long way." said William.

"It will give me the time to think." she said. "Oh, and William, before you go, take this."

She handed over the red journal. "It's yours now," she said.

"When you are ready, come and find me. OK?... But only when you are ready."

"Erm, ok," he said. "But don't you need it?"

"Remember, no 'erms', William.

Naturally, I have already made a copy. This one is now yours."

Cherri drove out of the drive and headed down the hill towards the village. William looked up at Jess's window, but her light was out.

Maybe I'll see her tomorrow, he thought.

The bloodied white robe did little to shield him from the cold wind now blowing in from the hills.

He walked back towards the house, praying that his family were fast asleep. There would be too many questions needing too many answers.

As he walked up the steps, there was a long shadow of someone blocking the light from the entrance hall.

The shadow of his bandaged head cast an odd shape onto the porch, like Frankenstein's monster. He was holding a massive double-barrelled shotgun.

"All dressed up and still alive, I see." said Grampy.

William had never been so happy to see someone before in his life. Grampy hugged him and wouldn't let him go. It reminded William of the time he fell off his bike when he was eight. As he did, he felt the tears well up, like someone was filling him up from his feet with hot water. Once they reached his neck, there was nothing he could do to stop them. William couldn't help thinking of the blood-soaked altar and all those hooded eyes, watching and waiting, waiting for him to be next.

"I heard your voice." he blubbed. "You... you told me to breathe."

"Shh, my boy, you are safe now." said Grampy.

He walked William into the house and sat him down at the kitchen table. He wiped the tears dry with the sleeves of the bloodied robe.

"What's with the old gun?" asked William.

"This is not just any old gun." said Grampy. "This here, is Berty." he said, unloading the cartridges and putting it away in a gun locker under the stairs. "I heard a car pull in, and you can't be too careful."

"I see you have my old journal? Now that will keep you up at night."

He went to a kitchen cabinet and pulled out a bottle of brandy, and two glasses.

"Berty? Strange name for a gun?" asked William.

"Almost as strange as his previous owner." Grampy said, with a smile. "But that's a long story for another time.

Cherri called me yesterday to explain what the plan was."

"And you agreed with it?" said William, with his anger starting to rise again.

"No... I was very angry with her for putting you so close to them, but I must agree.

Under these circumstances...it was the only way."

"Jacob, the main-" William started.

"THAT LITTLE PARRASITE!" Grampy interjected angrily, slamming the bottle down on the table. He sat opposite William, poured him a large brandy, and made him drink all of it.

Once he had calmed down slightly, Grampy said,

"Jacob...he was just a runt when I spared him. I thought it wasn't too late for him, I thought maybe he could change." Grampy stared out of the window, deep in thought. "We need to get you ready now, my boy," Grampy said, in a careful tone.

"Ready for what?" William asked.

"To fight!" he proclaimed. "They know who you are now, and there's no turning back. It's just a matter of time. The question is when they come, will you be ready and able?"

"From what I saw tonight, I will need to be." said William.

"But I'm not quite sure where to start." The warmth of the brandy started to build in his chest and calm him.

"Right at the beginning, William." Grampy smiled as he took a sip.

"The best ones always do." his green eyes twinkled, even in the low light, as he poured William another.

Printed in Great Britain
by Amazon